MARGARET SUTHERLAND

SAVING SHELBY SUMMERS

Complete and Unabridged

LINFORD
Leicester

First published in Great Britain in 2014

First Linford Edition
published 2015

All characters and events in this book are fictitious. Any resemblance to actual persons living or dead is strictly coincidental.

A catalogue record for this book is available from the British Library.

ISBN 978–1–4448–2516–9

Published by
F. A. Thorpe (Publishing)
Anstey, Leicestershire

Set by Words & Graphics Ltd.
Anstey, Leicestershire
Printed and bound in Great Britain by
T. J. International Ltd., Padstow, Cornwall

This book is printed on acid-free paper

SAVING SHELBY SUMMERS

At twenty-two, Shelby Summers is trying to understand why she attracts men who don't respect her. Her traumatic adolescence has left scars. How can she find romance with a loving partner? But then she is rescued from death by a mysterious stranger . . . Nathan Monroe, a rural vet, has moved to the city with his four-year-old daughter Caity, seeking to forge a new life. And when he offers Shelby a job as Caity's nanny, she dares to hope for the same . . .

Books by Margaret Sutherland
in the Linford Romance Library:

VALENTINE MASQUERADE
SEVEN LITTLE WORDS

To all the companion dogs who bring comfort to the lives of lonely people

1

Nathan Monroe parked his mud-splattered Nissan Patrol on the cliff top overlooking the beach and sat, looking down at the turmoil of whitecaps and hissing surf. The wild, lonely vista matched his mood. The past came with you, no matter how far you traveled.

Shrugging on his oilskin coat, he stepped out into the storm and stood facing the icy southerly. The wind whipped his brown hair as he strode to the cliff edge. Legs planted apart, arms hugging his chest, he was a dark, unapproachable figure, defiant in his stance. At the end of the beach, spray geysered high as waves smashed onto the rocks. Lashing rain, almost horizontal, stung his face and he pulled up the black hood. His vision was blurred as he squinted, peering downwards. Had he imagined movement on the beach? A vague shape interrupted the otherwise deserted vista. Large logs, washed up and rolled about by the ferocity of the current? Surely not a swimmer on such a day? An uneasy premonition gripped him. Instinctively he began to run downhill, digging the heels of his boots into the steep track to gain purchase as his stride lengthened.

His senses kicked in. He heard screams for help and saw the horse half-buried near the water line. The smeared rider, also caught in the sinkhole, was supporting the terrified animal's neck above the encroaching waves. The tide was coming in.

'Please help.' The boy sounded desperate. 'Help us!'

Nathan had reached the perimeter of the sand and the boy waved frantically. 'Get back! If you get caught, we'll all . . . '

'We'll have you both out in a jiffy.' Would he? Time was critical. Stay calm. His trained veterinary mind went into analytical mode. The Nissan's towing capacity would easily handle a horse weighing around four or five hundred kilograms. Fortunately he had heavy ropes. He'd even tossed his stun gun in with his vet case before driving down from Roma for the interview. He must get the four wheel drive down to the beach, get the horse roped, free the rider then use the vehicle to ease the horse free.

'Try not to panic. Talk to your horse. Keep him calm if possible. I'm bringing transport now.'

The boy's muddy features dissolved into terror at the prospect of being left alone. He was only a teenager, as far as Nathan could judge. The waves were already creeping closer. Would he have time to carry out a rescue? The thought of the boy and his horse vanishing from sight was too horrible to bear.

'Hang in there!' Turning, he sprinted toward the steep track. Was it the only vehicle access? He'd be at a forty five degree angle, and he had no time to consider tire pressure. Compelled by the plea of the trapped boy, he had to stop calculating and simply do it. Panting, he arrived at the Nissan, engaged the low range gear and took an involuntary deep breath as he went over the edge and the horizon disappeared.

Plunging down the steep slope, the Nissan angled sharply, on the verge of rolling. Nathan forced that image out of his head and concentrated on reaching the beach below. The tires slipped and skidded, the body swaying from side to side and lurching horribly as it hit buried logs and debris. Miraculously, he was on the beach, desperately seeking traction in the sand as he positioned the vehicle parallel to the shore. Jumping out, he grabbed ropes from the back and tossed them to the boy. He could see the muddy arm flail. Poor kid! This must be what pure terror felt like. The whites of the horse's eyes flashed as it struggled to break free.

'Hold on, fella!' Delivering the steady patter of words he'd so often used to calm a birthing cow or a sheep tangled in a barbed wire fence, Nathan shouted instructions.

'First one around your waist.' His deep voice resonated over the splash of breaking waves. The boy, concerned only with saving his companion, seemed about to disregard his order. He shouted again, louder, making the kid give a sob as he fumbled below the sludge, knotting his rescue line.

'Now the horse. Two loops and a reef knot. Can you reach under the belly?'

The boy obeyed, freeing his support of the animal's head. At once the animal panicked, fighting without any hope of freeing itself. A rogue wave swept in, splashing around the horse's mouth and into its flaring nostrils.

The next stage would be the hardest. Nathan would pull the kid out, but that would leave the horse alone. Unless the ropes held, it would be doomed to a slow horrible death. If it fought the pull of the vehicle too hard, it could fracture a delicate leg bone. What choice was there? It was one of those split-second moments when life either gave or took away.

'Ready?' He sprang into the driver's seat, engaged four wheel drive, and edged forward from the sand trap. Sensing the rider was being pulled free, the animal tried to follow, churning the filthy sludge in vain. Its whinny of fear was heart-rending. Nathan crept forward, drawing the sobbing figure onto firm sand. With shock he registered the fact that the rider was a girl, though, mud-covered as she was, it was only the vestiges of a bikini that gave her sex away as she stumbled upright, clutching the rope ends. Nathan grabbed the ropes and secured them to the tow bar.

'Do you have enough pulling power?' She sounded frantic.

'Sure will.' He had no idea whether the tires would grip, whether the ropes would break. He could only act, and hope the dreadful situation would not end in tragedy.

'Keep eye contact with the horse. Give me a signal if something seems to be going wrong. Ready?'

This was it. The rain had stopped. He hoped it was an omen. He checked he was in low range four wheel drive and eased forward, He wasn't a religious man, but he sent up something like a prayer.

There was huge resistance, then an awful sucking sound. Trembling and weak, the freed animal staggered onto firm-packed sand, allowing Nathan and the girl to exchange brief smiles of relief. Nathan grabbed a bucket from the boot and they gave the animal a cursory wash-down with seawater.

'Where do you live?' He was concerned for the rider, shivering half-naked in that unforgiving wind. He couldn't simply drive her home and leave the horse on the beach. It was in no state for riding. Someone would have to walk it back. It was a relief when she gestured toward a group of houses back from the cliff face, only a little further along the beach.

'He's not mine. I'm exercising him

for a friend while she's away on holiday. She rides him regularly on the beach. I thought it was safe.'

'You weren't to know. Look, you're cold. I've got some old gear in the vehicle. Better put something on.' He retrieved a bundle from the back.

The girl stared at a blood-stained flannel shirt and overalls.

'My working clothes,' Nathan explained.

She actually laughed. 'Right! What are you? A murderer?'

She'd just come from the very edge of death, and she had the resilience to make a joke? His admiration for the way she'd handled the crisis increased.

'Come on. Rug up.' Obediently she slipped her muddy arms into the garment he held for her, and pulled it close to cover her exposed breasts. Her nakedness was irrelevant. During life and death times the niceties of society were forgotten. All that mattered was survival.

The overalls were far too big. No matter. Side by side, leading the shocked horse, they walked the short distance toward the house she indicated. Here the cliff tapered to a gentle slope with well-marked vehicle access to the beach. It would be a lot easier driving out than it had been rocketing down that other pedestrian track. The girl paused for a moment to read the new-looking noticeboard, advising that conditions on the beach were treacherous due to recent storms.

'I didn't even see this.' She sounded self-reproachful. 'I was in a hurry, just dashed here, grabbed Blade and headed off.'

'Let's just be glad it ended okay. Go on in and shower. I'll stable Blade and have a look at those rope burns.'

He saw her teeth give an involuntary chatter. 'Get yourself warm. I'm not trained to treat human patients.'

But she stood her ground, her dark-blue eyes scanning his bearded face with an expression of amazement.

'You just saved my life. And Blade's. What can I do to thank you?'

Nathan shook his head, scattering raindrops from the dark hood of his coat.

'What about your four wheel drive?'

He gave her a gentle push. 'Get into the shower, then make us a hot drink. I'll be inside in a while.'

It took Nathan the better part of an hour to bring his vehicle up the access track, clean and settle the horse and treat the wounds where the rope had cut in. Fortunately the abrasions weren't deep. Blade's pulse and breathing had slowed to normal, and he was even looking around his stall for the prospect of feed. Nathan remembered the girl had said she was only minding him until her friend returned. She'd have a few hours' work on her hands when she was ready to give the horse a proper scrub and curry comb. The animal would do for now. Patting his flank reassuringly, Nathan left the stable and went back to the house. After a quick coffee he should get going. Not that he had anywhere to go. He'd only arrived in the city two days ago and had delayed arranging accommodation until he was sure of the locum's job. The interview yesterday had gone well enough to feel confident. He'd call in to the clinic and confirm things on Monday. Meantime, the good old Nissan served as his home.

He knocked several times, then let himself in quietly. The girl lay on the sofa, sound asleep. No wonder, she was exhausted. If he hadn't happened along, it would have ended very differently. As it was, no harm was done.

He stood gazing at her heart-shaped face with its small, straight nose and neatly curving eyebrows. She looked young and defenseless; her soft lips parted, her short black hair tumbled, her creamy complexion tinged with the blush pink of a rose. The toweling robe had fallen open, exposing the curve of one small, perfect breast that lifted and fell gently with each breath. She was lovely. To think that if he hadn't chanced to turn up . . . He took an involuntary breath, and stepped away. Moving quietly so as not to wake her, he placed a container on the table, and stood gazing down at her sleeping form. An expression of profound sadness crossed his face as he quietly let himself out of the house, revved up his engine, and drove away.

* * *

While she'd waited for the stranger to return, Shelby had taken his advice and headed straight for the shower. Her teeth chattered uncontrollably and shivers racked her body as shock and lowered body temperature took their toll. The hot water pouring over her was like a blessing, as she savored the caress of warmth trickling all the way to her extremities. Even after she'd washed her hair and soaped herself several times, she stayed, turning this way and that, feeling the stress of the past hours gradually subside.

She dried herself in the steamy air, and loosely knotted Jasmine's white bathrobe. Toweling her fine black hair, she combed it into the silky cap she wore, and helped herself to the perfumed talcum powder on the windowsill, needing to restore a feminine sense to the body so recently near extinction.

How could such a near-fatal accident occur? She'd ridden along that beach dozens of times in the past, whenever she'd driven out to visit her best friend. When she'd arrived at Jasmine's that afternoon, Blade had been restless. He was missing his owner and clearly begging for exercise. Shelby had decided to risk the leaden sky. A bracing canter along the tide line changed, in one moment, to fear, disbelief, then growing panic. The viscous mud sucked at her body. Her feet only just touched the bottom of the hole. Blade was in even deeper, in the center. She'd urged him, calling 'Up!' as she did when taking him over the low jumps in the paddock, but all that did was frighten the already disturbed animal. She remembered flailing, desperately trying to lever herself out of the sinkhole, while trying to keep the horse calm. Over and over she'd scanned the beach and cliff, wondering if any rescuer was in view. She'd been on the edge of death.

And he'd come.

Nameless. A dark, hooded figure, robbed of distinct features. She remembered the consolation of his deep voice and the confidence he'd inspired in her, even as she sank deeper, and the waves crept closer. She'd watched him run like an athlete to the cliff ascent. He'd risked his life in that headlong plunge to the beach when, surely, that swaying, rolling descent must end at any second in disaster.

Where was he now? He'd gone to get his Patrol and see to Blade. When he returned, she'd make sure he knew his bravery was appreciated. Meanwhile, her eyelids kept closing as though she could not fight off a powerful sedative. Turning the heater to full power, she curled up on the sofa. Oh, the things you took for granted! Being clean, and warm, and safe . . . She was alive! A wave of euphoria flooded her, and she smiled as her heavy eyelids closed.

But sleep only pulled her into a time tunnel to the past, and a place she never wanted to revisit. She was back in that nightmare of squealing rubber on the wet road, ugly voices, mocking laughter, the stench of beer and grease. Her struggles were ineffective as callous hands held her down and the fabric of her clothing ripped. Jasmine was screaming too. Or was that the police car siren, giving chase? Restless, she tossed and flailed, waking with a start as she rolled right off the narrow couch and landed on the floor.

Waking was almost worse than being in the dream. No! This couldn't be happening again. Her heart pounded, her palms were clammy, and every breath came so slowly and with such vise-like pressure that she was choking. She struggled upright.

I know what this is! I'm not dying, it's only a panic attack.

Now the present memory of her near-drowning was replacing that other, recurring nightmare. Convulsive shivers shook her body. She'd come so close to drowning. The bone-chilling cold, the relentless march of the tide, the horse's panic-stricken struggle to free himself from the oozing mud — none of this was a dream. Her aching muscles proved that. Her mind relived the rescue as the man appeared from nowhere. Like a dark angel he'd come, answering her desperate pleas, but would an angel have a handy four wheel drive?

Breathe! Slow and steady. That's right. In and out. This will pass. Remember, you've felt this way before and it always passed.

She'd been so sure she would never again suffer these symptoms, which had set in after the near-rape she'd suffered, and ruined her adolescence. Two naïve teenagers and a carload of drunken hoons had led to the violent attacks on

Jasmine and herself. Overnight, Shelby's happy life had been taken over by the panic syndrome that ruled five years of her adolescence. Critical years, spent in counseling and medical appointments, while her friends discovered the ropes of dating and social life. Jasmine seemed able to set the experience aside, moving on into jobs and romances. While Shelby stayed home. Hidden. Safe. Dependent, while other girls her age were confidently stepping out into the world.

Without her parents, she'd be a wreck. She owed them a positive return for all their faith and encouragement. Was it because she was an only child that they'd always been protective? Even so, they couldn't stop that one unwise impulse to hitchhike. They hadn't even reproached her for the thoughtless risk she and Jasmine had taken that day — over-confident teenagers, hitching a joyride. Her father just looked sorrowful. Her mother begged her never, ever to trust strangers in that way again. They'd coddled and nursed her back to health. If she ever spoke of travel, they suggested a supervised family trip to London or Paris. She owed them everything, yet some perverse need made her want to be independent. How nervous they'd been when she finally broke free, found a part-time job and moved in to share accommodation with several students in the city. To ease their worry, she'd promised to come home if the slightest problem troubled her.

Two years, now. And she'd been fine. Fine! She mustn't make too much of one episode. After all, anyone would panic after nearly drowning.

The symptoms were starting to ease. She must get up. It was evening, already dark, except for the glow of the heater. Her head throbbed. She needed to go to the bathroom and to make a hot drink. There might be painkillers in the medicine cabinet to ease her headache. She found the light switch and looked around, wondering if by magic the stranger might be somewhere in the room. She hadn't meant to fall asleep. Who was he? Where had he come from? He'd been a savior in that unstable, churning world. Coolly judging, calmly deciding what to do, he'd risked his safety to ensure hers.

The near-drowning was no illusion, and neither was the man. She checked out the room. Yes, he'd been in the cottage while she slept, and he'd even left some antibiotic powder for Blade. But no note. No name or phone number. Shelby didn't care. He'd rescued her.

She eyed the telephone. The urge to rush home to her parents was still strong. A quick call, and they would come and take her home to her childhood bedroom. How clearly she could see its pale blue walls, the storybooks lined along the white-painted shelf, and the teddy bear pajama case propped against soft pillows, his button eyes calmly gazing out at nothing. She'd been so sure she'd seen the last of these attacks. Her confidence plummeted. Sometimes the world was just too hard a place. But still she refused to make the phone call that would mean she'd failed. Her illness would have won, and she would always be a special case, a delicate daughter who could not make it alone.

Her stomach growled and she thought longingly of her mother's home-made soup and buttered toast, carried to her on a tray by her father. She rummaged in the fridge and found cheese and bread. No way was she returning to that shared house tonight. The tenants kept changing, and the present lot were loud and messy, though good-natured enough. No, Jasmine would be home in the morning. Better to confide in the friend who knew her background. She wouldn't overreact. Anyone would be freaked out, surely, by such a horrible experience. And, Shelby needed to share the story of the mysterious stranger who'd come out of nowhere and saved her life.

In the bathroom, she brushed her short black cap of shiny hair and smoothed moisturizer on her creamy skin. What a contrast to the earlier wild-haired, semi-naked figure! Had the man rushed off because he couldn't stand the sight of her? She kicked aside the heap of filthy clothes she'd discarded. The shirt and overalls he'd given her on the beach lay in a sodden heap, their bloodstained condition suggesting he was a hands-on man with traumas and emergencies. She'd wash the clothing and take it home with her. Surely Fate would draw them together again?

Gradually her disappointment at the return of the panic syndrome faded and her heart filled with gratitude. The man wasn't just a savior, he was a soul mate. Who was he? He'd carried ropes and veterinary equipment. Clearly he must be a vet, though anyone less like a professional man she'd never seen. The hooded stranger had settled in her memory as an archetypal form, appearing when hope seemed to be gone. One thing only, she knew; whoever this savior was, he'd rescued her from certain death. Oh, she wanted to thank him, to repay him, somehow. But as quickly as he'd come, he'd disappeared. Racking her brains, she could not even remember if he'd told her his name. Somewhere, somehow, she would see him again.

* * *

When Jasmine arrived home from her fortnight holiday in Cairns, she was surprised to see Shelby's Yaris still parked outside the unit. Bursting to share the news that her long-term boyfriend had proposed and given her a beautiful engagement ring, she bounced through the door to find Shelby still huddled in bed. Jasmine stared at her friend in shock.

'What's happened? You look terrible!'

'I feel terrible! Aching all over. Every breath hurts.'

Jasmine sat on the edge of the bed. Now what had gone wrong? Shelby was so pale. The smudges under her eyes reminded Jasmine of their teen years, before Shelby got sick, when they'd briefly adopted Goth fashions.

'What are these bruises on your arms? Has someone attacked you? Don't tell me one of those juveniles at the share house . . . ' Shelby did have a way of trusting the wrong people. Just last year she'd fallen for an Internet sob story — someone supposedly dying of cancer — and lost most of her savings. You'd think she would have learned after their hitchhiking disaster. Jasmine had toughened right up after that. Shelby had tried to follow her advice and adopt a cautious manner, but at heart she still seemed to think everyone was as kind and gentle as she was.

'Of course not. I was riding Blade on the beach. We hit a sinkhole. I nearly drowned.'

'Oh no!' As Shelby recounted the story, Jasmine listened in horror.

No wonder Shell looked so wrung out. Tears were spilling down her cheeks.

'Hey, don't cry.' Jasmine squeezed her friend's hand. 'Has a doctor checked you out? Maybe something's broken.'

'It's not the pain. I had another panic attack, Jaz. I was so sure they were over.'

'You haven't had one of those for years, have you? Has it passed now?'

'Yes.' Shelby managed a smile as she indicated the sparkling ring on Jasmine's finger. 'Come on! When are you going to tell me the details?'

'Not till I've made you some lunch. You get dressed and we'll eat outside. You'll feel better in the sunshine.'

'I'll have to borrow some gear.' Fortunately the girls were both petite and often exchanged personal belongings and clothes.

They ate soup and sandwiches on the small terrace overlooking the beach. The sea was calm, a deep glittering blue punctuated with frilly whitecaps. People were jogging or strolling along the sand, throwing sticks for their dogs. A few intrepid surfers were pursuing the big swells further out from shore. Impossible to think it was the same place where Shelby had come so close to losing her life.

The sun was out, catching the facets of Jasmine's diamond ring. Rob's proposal was no surprise, really. She'd been going with him for years. But concern for Shelby made her reticent. Rob was going to New Zealand to investigate a job, and Jasmine planned to go with him. It wouldn't be easy to say goodbye. Shelby had been through a lonely time, when school friends had drifted away, embarrassed by her strange condition and withdrawn manner.

'I'm so happy for you.' Shelby sounded sincere. 'Tell me the full story.'

Jasmine was happy to talk about her romantic getaway, but when they moved on to the story of Shelby and her rescuer, Jasmine had trouble believing the facts.

'You're telling me a seven foot tall stranger drove off the cliff to save you?'

'It's true! If you don't believe me, go and look at the rope burns on Blade. We need to check him out and see if he needs a vet. That's why I stayed overnight.' She corrected herself. 'Actually, I couldn't face going back to the house.'

'I can imagine.' Jasmine had visited a few times. The place would be a mess from Justin and his mates, partying. Loud music, beer cans and chip packets. It might have worked for Shelby at the beginning, when the tenants had been girls who did their share of the housework. Living with a bunch of young students was crazy.

Jasmine's cell phone rang and she checked the caller, her ring glinting in the sun.

'Rob?' Waving, she went off to talk privately to her fiancé and to visit the stable, where Blade nuzzled her. With a pang she realized she would have to find him a new owner if the New Zealand job eventuated. But you couldn't stay in a rut all your life.

'I'll find you a loving owner.' She blew gently into his nostrils and he flicked his ears appreciatively. 'You and Shelby will be fine, Blade.'

Determined to focus on her future, she saddled Blade and coaxed the horse into a gentle walk along the cliff road.

2

The phone was running hot as an athletic-looking man in his late twenties arrived at Pelican Waters Veterinary Clinic. Shelby frowned. Already three clients were ahead of him and there certainly didn't seem to be anything wrong with his energetic, half-breed black pup. She'd returned to work on Monday, and was bearing the brunt of the short staffing since the trained vet nurse had resigned and Melanie, the third partner, was away on her extended honeymoon overseas.

Shelby checked the bookings. His must just be a casual visit. His undisciplined dog was showing no sign of illness as it bounded on large puppy paws toward a panicked cat in a carry basket. Shelby spoke briskly as the man approached the desk.

'There'll be a long wait this morning.

I can make you an appointment for this afternoon?'

'It's okay. I'm in no hurry.'

The resonant timbre of his voice gave her a shock. He sounded like the man on the beach. But her rescuer had been so tall, and darkly bearded. This guy was clean-shaven, just under six feet in height, and his thick, wavy hair was mid-brown. In his blue-and-white checked shirt, jeans and elastic-sided boots, he was more an R. M. Williams' outback figure than her mysterious hero. He smiled, maintaining direct eye contact as though trying to place her from somewhere. She did not respond to the question in his intelligent eyes, or the tilt of his smile. Her morning had been anything but funny. The routine appointments had been totally disrupted when two emergencies arrived at once; a spaniel hit by a car, and a terrier that had ingested snail bait. The two rostered vets were flat out in the treatment rooms. The practice owner, Trevor Blake, was attending to the gastric lavage and Judy, the second vet, was assessing the dislocated hip. As for the displaced clients — patience was running thin as their pets paced, whined or hissed their displeasure.

'There'll be at least an hour's delay. We have emergencies.'

She glanced away, meaning to convey they had no spare time, but the man took no notice; just stood there, staring at her oddly. For some reason, her stomach twisted.

She spoke sharply. 'Weigh your dog over there and take a seat. As you can see, there's a queue.'

The phone rang. A frantic owner had found a tick lodged inside the ear of her dog. The animal was off its food and vomiting.

'Bring your dog in straight away.'

Another real emergency! Shelby addressed the restless waiting room.

'Our vets are likely to be tied up for quite a while. It might be better if you re-book.'

Nobody moved. In a few minutes the

nine-thirty appointment would arrive. Shelby snatched up the phone and tried to cancel. No answer. Too late. Trevor was calling from the back room.

'Shelby, I could use some assistance here.'

The head vet sounded peremptory and she sighed. It was impossible to man the reception desk and help in the treatment room at the same time.

The man with the black dog was still standing at the desk.

'I can pop this fellow in a cage and lend a hand, if you like.'

Shelby stared. The man made her acutely uncomfortable. Something about his voice . . .

'Our staff are properly trained vets.' She spoke dismissingly.

'So am I. Nathan Monroe. The new locum. Just introducing myself and taking a look around. Looks like you could use an extra pair of hands.'

Why hadn't he said anything? He looked okay but . . .

'Where are your credentials?'

He raised his eyebrows. 'I'm sure Trevor can vouch for me. He interviewed me last Friday for the job.'

Stubbornly she nodded. 'Follow me then. He's working on a dog.'

Within a few minutes, Nathan had been cleared and welcomed. She was glad when he caged his dog and went to a consulting room, out of her sight. She went on with her duties in an automatic way. It was uncanny, the way he reminded her of that mysterious figure on the beach. And why did his gaze cause that strange twisting deep in her belly?

By eleven a.m. the waiting room was empty. The sick animals were sleeping in recovery while the operating vets had stripped off their overalls and were preparing to relax over morning tea.

Shelby looked in the consulting room where Nathan had removed the tick, and was outlining treatment to the worried owner.

'Will you join us for coffee?'

She felt embarrassed now. She'd

cross-examined him like a criminal. Perhaps he'd thought it was funny, pretending he was a client. Why not simply explain who he was? She didn't need a practical joker or any other kind of trickster in her life. Naiveté left scars, as the weekend had reminded her.

The new vet joined them, leaning back in the chair and stretching out his legs as though hosting a relaxed get together. Shelby quietly observed, thinking how quickly first impressions formed. Even in the chaos when he'd arrived at the clinic, she'd somehow noted those salient features — fit athletic build, medium height, and competent manner. He moved with an agreeably loose air. There was nothing formal about Nathan Monroe. It seemed he was from a rural veterinary background and the other vets were curious, tossing him questions about his past experience.

Subtly checking him out again, she tried to analyze her unsettled state. She couldn't seem to control her urge to stare at him, almost as though she was memorizing his features — alert hazel eyes, a firm mouth, sloping shoulders tapering down to a lean waist, jeans sitting low on hard-looking hips. Yes, he was the type to leap a wire fence and stride into a paddock to confront a recalcitrant bull or frisky stallion. So why apply for work in a small animal clinic like Pelican Waters?

He was doing it again! Catching her eye and quirking the corners of his mouth, as though they shared some secret. Quickly she lowered her gaze and sipped her cooling coffee. Her system was out of sorts, on edge. She felt strangely hot. Was she flushed? Perhaps her soaking over the weekend was turning into a cold? She was definitely feeling . . . What? Whatever it was, she didn't like it.

She didn't like men. The years she'd spent, physically and emotionally damaged, had turned her right off. Her broken arm and Jasmine's concussion had healed, but not so the emotional price of near-rape. Even when she finally found the courage to leave home, her odd choice of accommodation made sense to her. She was safe with her immature flat-mates. The present lot were good-natured, beer-drinking, footie-watching guys who treated her like one of the boys. But as usual, Jasmine was right. It was time to move on. Apart from a dog or two, she would be happier on her own.

Nathan was speaking directly to her. 'It gets pretty busy here. Do you double as receptionist and nurse?'

'What?' Her mind had wandered off and she blushed.

'We've had a staff reshuffle recently,' Trevor explained when she didn't answer. 'One of our vets married and left the practice, and on top of that, our veterinary nurse resigned. Shelby's learning the ropes of basic procedures like dental scaling and wound dressings, as well as handling the front desk. Of course there are limits to her skills. We're advertising now for a trained nurse.'

'Sounds full on. Does promotion pay well?' Nathan was speaking directly to her. How should she reply? Trevor had stressed her good fortune in extending her skills, but he ran the practice in a thrifty way. No pay raise had been mentioned. She stared into her cup.

'I'm not worth a raise,' she mumbled.

Had she really said that, and in such a negative tone?

All three of the vets were staring at her, expressions mirroring their surprise. With a wry smile, she stood up and collected the empty cups.

'Guess I've got the grumps today. Not much sleep last night.'

She'd returned to her shared house, but opted to keep the beach episode to herself. If only the memory would go away. Was this another freak episode to haunt her forever? She wanted the dark, hooded rescuer out of her head for good.

'Here, let me.' Nathan had jumped to his feet and was reaching to take the dishes to the sink. Shelby felt an insane urge to reach out and stroke the curling golden hairs on his sinewy forearm. His hands looked strong yet gentle. But the wedding ring . . . An unaccountable feeling of disappointment confused her. Why would she care if the new vet was married? Was she losing it? She ought to be checked out by a doctor.

'Don't bother. I can do it.' She spoke sharply. The further away from this man she was, the better. She didn't want any help from anyone. Especially him.

Still standing, Nathan gave a bemused shrug. 'I might push off now. I'm checking in to a motel while I sort out a house to rent.'

'Do you have anything specific in mind?' asked Judy.

'I want to rent out of town. What's Maitland like? I'm looking for a country outlook, horses, cattle . . . '

'The area's lovely, but a fair bit of travel every day.'

Nathan laughed. 'I'm a rural vet, remember? I'm used to distances and I love driving. I always feel I'm off on an adventure when I'm in the driver's seat.'

Trevor stood up and stretched. 'Better check my patient's clotting factors. I think we caught him just in time.' The senior vet shook Nathan's hand. 'Good thing you dropped by today. We appreciate your help.'

'You're welcome. I'll collect my pup and push off now.' He waved to Judy, who was obviously taken with his friendly manner. She beamed at him.

'I noticed your four wheel drive in the parking lot,' she said. 'You won't have much call for an off-road vehicle in the city.'

'We'll see. I don't plan to vegetate at home.'

He was deliberately avoiding speaking to Shelby. She tried to think of a way to counteract her abrupt refusal of his help.

'What's your dog's name?' It was all she could bring out. Her mouth felt dry as his intelligent gaze locked on to hers.

'He's just a stray. You can see by his

condition. No collar and he's not even microchipped.'

'Where did you find him?'

'He found me.' He gave a cheerful laugh. 'His manners leave a lot to be desired. He's going to need a few lessons at that puppy school you run.'

Her warning bells sounded. Had he been doing research on her? Predators came in all disguises. Weren't her parents always reminding her to be careful? She hadn't dared tell them how she'd been sucked in to that Internet scam last year.

'How do you know I run a puppy school?' she demanded.

'I read the notice on the front desk. The one with your photo that says 'Puppy School'.' He sounded mildly puzzled.

Shelby wanted to counteract her rudeness. He'd only made a friendly comment, after all.

'Can you have your dog at the motel? Usually they aren't permitted.'

'I'll have to lock him in the car.

Hardly ideal. Not when he starts barking at midnight!' He brushed back a lock of unruly brown hair.

'I could take him home for you. There's a yard. It would only be for a few days, wouldn't it?'

'Hopefully, yes. I'm inspecting a few rental places tomorrow.' Nathan hesitated. 'It's going to be difficult at the motel. Sure you don't mind?'

'I love dogs.' She spoke firmly. 'He shouldn't be locked in a car. He's only a pup.'

'In that case, thanks. I appreciate it. I'll get him out of your hair now. Should I drop him at your house this evening?'

'No, just bring him here. I have a puppy class at four.'

For some reason, she didn't want Nathan to meet Justin and his drunken mates. She'd made a mess of the whole encounter with him, from the moment he'd walked through the door. There was no need to round it off looking like a prize idiot.

'You work hard,' he commented.

Shelby shrugged. 'It's expected,' she said. 'I'll get your dog.'

* * *

Nathan loaded his pup in the back seat, swung aboard the dusty Nissan Patrol and revved the engine, his enthusiastic manner that of a crusader urging his steed into battle. He and the old rust bucket had clocked up three hundred thousand kilometers. Together they'd negotiated off-road tracks, flooded ditches and the endless red dirt roads of the outback. Driving around the sedate city of Newcastle didn't compare.

Although his start had been anything but sedate. That near-drowning on the beach had taken every scrap of his initiative. The shocking image of the distraught girl and the horse would stay in his memory forever. At the time, he'd simply followed his instincts. It had been uncanny; almost as though he'd had a chance to reclaim his wife from the wild torrent of floodwater that had swept her away five months ago.

He knew Samantha was gone. He just couldn't believe it. She was always there — in his dreams, calling him, her arms wide open to him, and in his nightmares, as the flooded vehicle tipped and she was taken. Sometimes she was the fun-loving girl he'd first met on her holiday, tramping and mountain-climbing in the Mount Egmont National Park near his parents' farm in New Zealand. He'd followed her back to Australia, hoping to persuade her to marry and return home with him, but he was the one to make the move across the Tasman to be with her. His veterinary qualification from Massey University was looked on well in Australia. He'd worked in several practices, moving around at first, enjoying the variety of rural work with horses, cattle and pigs. That suited Sam. She'd loved riding, mustering, the whole bit. She was happy when he took on a permanent position near Roma, in Queensland. A family girl, Sam often flew across to Gympie to see her parents. The birth of Caity, four years ago, had set the seal on a committed relationship for them.

Nathan swerved and gestured to the tow-truck driver who'd cut in front of him without signaling. If the fellow wanted a race he could have one. Gunning the powerful engine of his four wheel drive, he surged forward with a satisfying burst of speed. Thinking back to romantic campfires under the stars was just a waste of time. Those had been good years. Now they were over. All he could do was try and make a new life for his daughter. As a temporary measure, Caity was with his mother-in-law. But Nathan knew he couldn't parent a child and cover the broad territory of a rural vet. He'd had to give away the job he loved, accepting that Caity deserved a proper home with him. How 'proper' he wasn't sure. He could only hope his parenting skills would be adequate. Reports from Barbara, his daughter's grandmother, made him uneasy. She said Caity wasn't coping with the loss of her mother. And Barbara herself was finding the responsibility far too much for her health. He needed a younger nanny or housekeeper — someone able to handle the problems of a grieving little girl. Probably a woman in Samantha's own age bracket, under thirty.

Nathan was determined to do all in his power for Caity. That was why he'd rescued the stray pup. She'd love to play with him. And the house he was inspecting was near a riding school. She'd like that.

One thing at a time. At least the job was secure. How he'd handle small animal practice remained to be seen. Pampered pooches and white mice weren't exactly his forte.

He eased back on the accelerator when the tow-truck swerved off on a side road, recalling how he'd walked into the surgery and come face to face with the miniature Amazon at the front desk. What was her name? Shelby Summers. For one crazy moment, he'd been certain she was the girl he'd rescued on the beach. He could vividly summon his last image before he crept away — a sleeping beauty, open and yielding, her dark hair and creamy skin reminding him so much of his wife.

Clearly he'd been deluded. In fact the whole episode had been unreal. The fierce little receptionist was nothing like Samantha. He recalled the way she'd glared at him, straight black fringe sweeping sapphire blue eyes — on guard, like Xena the Warrior Princess. Wary as she was, she'd shot a few verbal arrows his way. Yet, in the tea room, he saw a different person. Low self-esteem, somehow lonely. How did he know that? Like recognized like, that was how.

That pushy driver was overtaking him again! Had he taken a shortcut? Nathan welcomed the distraction from his thoughts. This was one way to pass the journey out to the real estate office in Maitland. His search at the Internet café had located just the kind of house he liked. He'd pay the deposit and pick up the key to the old farmhouse, then see what furniture came with the place. Vacant for years, the agent had admitted. Pretty rundown. But after viewing pictures of city apartments with their minute en-suites and phony balconies, Nathan needed a familiar place to start his new life. How many rural homes like the one in this photo had he entered over the years? Called out to diagnose bloat or deliver a lamb, he'd be invited back to the friendly kitchen for a feed and friendly conversation. His kind of folk, his kind of life.

The tow-truck driver conceded defeat and dropped back. Nathan turned on the radio and pushed a well-used tape into the deck. As Handel's Hallelujah burst forth, he accelerated and added his rich tenor to the chorus. Life wasn't all bad. Maybe things would sort out. He just had a feeling this move was right.

* * *

Time flew when the clinic was busy. Afternoons could drag sometimes. Shelby ran a load of wash, turned on the sterilizer and cleaned out vacated cages as owners picked up their pets after their day surgery. She hoped Trevor found a replacement vet nurse soon. He kept delaying her holiday leave. It was a bit much, expecting Shelby to handle Reception plus act as a stand-in when struggling animals had to be restrained for nail clipping or tablet administration. Trained nurses knew how to monitor anesthesia or carry out simple dental scaling. Those were duties Shelby had managed to avoid so far. She disliked the sight of blood and witnessing operations made her feel faint. Trevor laughed at her squeamishness and assured her she'd get over it. She didn't think so. Her skills lay in the area of puppy handling and general training.

If the new vet expected her to perform any gross procedures, she would set him straight. He seemed easy-going. It was true that he had a likeness to the man on the beach, so that her first emotions had been disbelief, joy, and then disappointment. Now that she'd settled down, she thought he'd be easy to work with. It was hardly his fault that she desperately wanted to see her rescuer again and thank him properly.

As the clock hands approached four o'clock, she felt her spirits lift. Half a dozen owners and their pets were booked for her training session. With such young dogs, she liked to keep things low key, making the occasion something everyone enjoyed. Socializing the puppies was important to start at eight weeks, if problems were to be prevented before bad habits set in. A dog with behavior problems could be hard to handle. Often, owners succumbed to the charm of a cute puppy, only to find six months later that a large, unruly animal dominated their lives.

As Shelby's training method encouraged positive reinforcement with rewards, the classes were happy occasions. She quickly picked out the type of owner who thought punishment worked, and corrected that approach. But at puppy class they were few and far between. Owners who bothered to attend were usually responsible and were willing to put in the time to have an obedient pet.

Meeting and greeting, walking on a leash, sitting and lying down were the pups' goals for the six week course. As dogs paid little attention to size, it was often amusing to see a large pup like a Rottweiler backing away from a feisty terrier or Chihuahua. Shelby was explaining the signs of an anxious dog when she saw Nathan come through the door with his pup. He stood quietly, observing the friendly activity as owners asked questions, trotted their pets in a circle, and gave the hand signal to lie down.

The class was over. The attendees filed out, thanking her, and Nathan congratulated her.

'You work very confidently with the

class. Well done!'

Her face warmed at his praise. He was looking at her curiously.

'Shelby, was it you at the beach on Saturday?'

Slowly she nodded. 'I've been wondering too. I don't understand. You're not the man I remember!'

'In what way?' His tone was gentle.

'He was very tall, and dark, and he had a beard.'

'Well, I'm having the same trouble recognizing you. We met in such unnatural conditions. It was pouring, you were covered in muddy sand, I was in a black oilskin and I probably looked so tall to you because you were buried in that hole. As for the beard, Trevor hinted it gave me an unprofessional look so I shaved it off.'

'Typical Trevor!' Shelby nodded as she looked him up and down as though he was an exhibit in a gallery. Now she understood the strange connection she'd felt when he first arrived at the clinic, and the odd looks he'd kept giving her. So here he was in the flesh, the hero of her dreams. Except that Nathan Monroe was just a decent ordinary man with a wedding ring on his finger. Standing near him was giving her goosebumps. Her fingers strayed to stroke the black pup, who gave her hand a friendly lick.

'How did it go with the house-hunting?' she asked.

'It's done. The agent will find out if the owner wants to collect his belongings. I can pick up the key tomorrow and prepare to move in by the weekend. Can you handle Skip till then?'

Shelby smiled. 'You've named him?'

'Temporarily. Probably Tearaway would suit him better.'

'I can bring him out to your place if you like.'

Nathan looked pleased. 'Great. You can inspect my new house. Down, Skip!' The pup's boisterous affection had almost knocked Shelby off her feet. 'Sorry about that. He's on the wild side.'

'A good walk will fix that. Want to

join me, before I take him home?'

'If you're not in a hurry?'

In fact, the beach episode had left her drained and exhausted. 'A walk will clear my mind,' was all she said. She turned off the lights and locked the clinic. It was late June, already growing dark. Trees were silhouetted against the pale sky, where pink clouds hung in swathes. Streetlights flickered and came on as they walked side by side. Skip welcomed the chance to explore. He dashed back and forth, exploring the intoxicating scents.

Shelby liked walking the dog with Nathan. The fading light created an atmosphere of intimacy but conversation was another matter. She was still coming to terms with the beach accident, and her mistaken impression of her hero. She felt embarrassed, knowing he'd seen her half-naked, filthy and distraught. Nathan didn't volunteer any information, either. They walked briskly, allowing Skip to set the pace. Nathan seemed to be a million miles away.

'How's the horse?' he asked, as though he'd been racking his brains for something to say.

'Good. His abrasions look clean. My friend and I gave him a thorough grooming on Sunday. Jasmine even took him for a short ride. I don't think he's suffered any after-effects.'

'Great.'

There was a scent of recently-cut grass in the air. The roosting birds twittered in the branches above them. Skip dawdled beside a litter bin, entranced by the promise of an empty milk shake carton. Hysterical yaps suddenly rent the air as a stout white bulldog in one of the gardens spotted Skip. He escaped through a gate, pursued by an elderly man. Skip took off in pursuit, towing Shelby behind him while Nathan dodged cars, finally managing to catch the runaway. He scooped up the heavy, struggling dog and returning it to its owner, then helped Shelby bring Skip under control. They looked at each other, panting a little, and laughing.

'You're quite the white knight, aren't you!'

Nathan's teeth flashed a smile. 'I have my moments.'

'So does your dog! You'll have to get him into training.'

Nathan agreed. 'I hope he won't frighten Caity. This bloke's going to be big, judging by the size of his paws.'

'Your wife's nervous of dogs?' She'd somehow expected a country vet's wife to be well used to them.

Nathan's voice was distant as he spoke. 'Caity is my daughter.'

Abruptly he turned back toward the clinic, obviously not intending to continue the walk. Shelby had to hurry to keep up with him. Nathan did not speak again until they reached the parking lot, where Shelby's red Yaris was. Skip whined as he was bundled aboard, along with a bag of dog food, and Nathan patted his head.

'We'll be settled in a few days. Hang in there,' he said, checking the fitted barrier was firmly in position before closing the back door and nodding to Shelby. 'Thanks again for minding him.'

'No problem.' If she'd upset him in some way, he wasn't intending to explain.

Going their separate ways, the two vehicles headed into the traffic stream. Shelby felt a familiar sinking of her heart as she turned onto her street and saw the old eight-cylinder cars randomly pulled up on the overgrown grass. Jason's mates were visiting again. Inside the house, the monotonous beat of rap music echoed from open windows. She could imagine beer cans everywhere and the day's dishes all over the countertop. Worst of all would be the expressions when she complained. It was like coming home to a family of resentful teenagers. Why did Jason allow it? On his own, he wasn't too bad. He simply reverted to childhood when his mates were there to urge him on. He knew how she felt about them.

At least there were no complaints

when she arrived home with Skip.

The visitors made a fuss over the pup, in the way of young men who lived for today and did not think about the responsibilities and ties of taking in a pet. She watched as Jason and the others petted the hungry pup, feeding him chips and offering him beer in a dish. She knew their attention span would wane quickly, and Skip would be relegated to the sidelines. How many pets like him waited in shelters, their usefulness as a novelty outlived?

Skip was lucky. Nathan would provide the care and training the dog needed. Perhaps the pup could start with puppy class, although he was already half-grown. Another option could be the local dog-training grounds. Shelby knew a few of the volunteer trainers there, and approved of their methods.

Why had Nathan terminated their walk so abruptly when she'd mentioned his wife? Perhaps they were separated, or divorced? Whatever the situation, it was obviously a forbidden topic with the vet. He was friendly enough and obviously strong in an emergency, yet she sensed painful issues in his life. Well, everybody had those.

The music was too loud. She tipped biscuits into Skip's bowl and filled a dish with water. He could sleep in her room tonight. She didn't want to tether him outside, where he could dig up plants, bark, and probably escape onto the busy road.

Closing her door, she spread an old blanket on the floor and sat on her bed, stroking his head. His solemn brown eyes gazed back at her and a tear slipped down her cheek. She felt closer to this stray mutt than she did to any of her flat mates. It was time to move out, but the logistics of finding new accommodations felt overwhelming. When Skip curled up on her feet, she let him stay. He was company and somehow made her feel less alone. At present her life felt unsettled. The accident on the beach seemed to remind her of all her worst insecurities. If Jasmine's fiancé took the job in New Zealand, it was a sure thing that Shelby was about to lose her best friend. She was also disappointed in her job. She hadn't thought it through, imagining a vet clinic would be a happy environment to work in. Of course there were the enjoyable moments, but often she was faced with suffering, neglect and pain. Her home life gave her no respite. She felt taken for granted, by Jason, by the head vet, yet lacked the courage to make a stand.

Tossing and turning, she only fell into a deep sleep near morning, and woke with a headache. Avoiding breakfast, she fed Skip and tethered him on a long rope in the yard.

There was no sign of Jason or the others. They were probably nursing hangovers, camped out on the floor somewhere. She scribbled a quick note, reminding them to keep the gate shut while the dog was visiting. It wasn't a good feeling, knowing you couldn't rely on people.

Her day at work started badly. As she went through the back entrance, a trail of blood and a canvas body bag raised a sick feeling in her stomach. Another life abruptly ended. In a side room, she could hear the sound of sobbing.

'Morning, Shelby.' Even Trevor sounded sorry. 'Road accident, I'm afraid. Nothing we could do. Perhaps you can take the lady a cup of tea?'

But within a few minutes, the vet was absorbed in his next consultation. He was lucky, Shelby thought. You could only stomach this work if you could maintain a distance. Witnessing the distraught owner's heartbreak, Shelby almost broke down herself. She knew she was too soft, but how could you harden your heart? As she answered phones and took bookings, the presence of the deceased animal stayed with her. Knowing Skip had been left in the dubious care of irresponsible young men wasn't helping either. She wasn't cut out for this work. The only part of it she liked was the puppy schooling.

The day dragged endlessly. She was thankfully preparing to leave the clinic when Trevor stopped her at the door. He seemed oblivious to the morning's sad outcome.

'Shelby, I'm just letting you know we have inventory review again next month. You'll be required to work that weekend.'

A burst of resentment tightened her breathing.

'Again? Why? We've just done one for the end of June. I may not be available.'

Trevor gave no explanation and ignored her words. 'It's part of the job, and it certainly can't be done during clinic hours. I'll let you know the day.'

He turned and walked away. His request made no sense to her.

Required to work? No please or thank you? No mention of extra pay?

She slammed the door as she left the clinic. Even the traffic was against her. Every light was red. Roadwork slowed the home-bound queue of cars, and she passed a nasty-looking accident where an ambulance was parked, lights flashing.

She arrived home and sighed. Jason's mates were there, as usual. At least the gate was firmly latched. Skip, untied from his rope, greeted her like a long-lost friend. But her smile didn't last when she saw the empty Kentucky Fried Chicken boxes scattered all over the lawn. Surely they hadn't given him the carcasses? She'd seen enough pets with cooked bones lodged in their throat or gut to be worried.

A confrontation with boozy young men felt beyond her. The problem would have to be addressed. Just not now. Clipping on Skip's lead she set off for a brisk walk. The fading sky of an Australian winter reminded her of walking with Nathan yesterday. Such an ordinary thing to do. Just a man, a woman, and a dog. Not a lot to say, yet enough to make her feel complete, somehow. He wasn't into formality but she sensed he was reliable. He might not be that unreal hero of her imagination, but she had to admit he was an attractive man. That impulse to reach out and touch the springy hair on his arm was just an instinct, the way one's fingers were drawn to sift through the soft fur of a cat. Good thing he had a family. She didn't know how to cope with available men.

Skip strained ahead, lured by the mysterious messages left for him by other canines. She ought to call him to heel, as training required, but today she hadn't the strength even to discipline a dog. Her heart thudded as she rehearsed the scene waiting for her back at Jason's. She couldn't rightly order his friends to leave. It was his place, as much as hers.

Crossing the small suburban park, she came to a slatted seat and sank down in the fading light. Forced-back tears constricted her throat. Sensing her mood, Skip trotted back to rest his head on her knee. Shelby stroked his silky ears.

'I'll have to move out,' she told him. It was just another situation gone wrong. Nothing to get too upset about.

Her casual friendship with Jason was hardly mind-blowing. He was someone to go home to, that was all.

That wasn't quite true. The first couple of months had been fun. His youth and impetuous ideas had made her laugh. It seemed you left a tiny part of yourself behind when you walked away. She was starting to wonder whether her damaged heart would ever heal. Her chest felt overcrowded, as though breathing took up all the space where her heart should be.

Picking up the lead, she set off for home. Calmer now, Skip obeyed her body signals, coming to a stand on the curb and heeling nicely as they crossed the road. If only you could train people so easily! One day, perhaps in ten years' time, Jason might be a more considerate man. But she wouldn't be around to see that.

Her mind made up, she walked back to the house.

3

Country air always smelled clean, even when the breeze carried hints of manure along with jasmine, honeysuckle and the scent of warm dry grass. Not trusting the rickety planks that bridged the ditch, Nathan left his four wheel drive parked at the roadside and walked toward the old farmhouse he'd just rented. In his pocket he carried the keys and lease papers to his new home. The agent certainly hadn't led him to expect a palace, but the old place had a certain rustic charm. Inhaling deep and happy breaths, Nathan walked up cracked steps and thrust his key in the door. It gave easily, as though welcoming anyone who cared to come inside.

A brief inspection satisfied him. Yes, this house would do. It was the right place to bring his daughter, this rambling home with its view of horses and cattle and drifting willows edging the boundary creek. Caity would heal here, and hopefully so would he. His present feeling of loss was still too keen to plan any future.

The agent had said any remaining fittings were his to dispose of or use as he liked. He wasn't worried about the old-fashioned décor. It would do until he was ready to sell his large acreage up north. Before he invested in a suitable property to raise Caity, he needed to sort out schools, transport, and her general care.

Over the next few days he would organize some basic services. Having checked out the rooms more thoroughly, he listed essentials needed to make the old house habitable. An electrician would need to check the elements and repair the wiring, where the number of mice droppings suggested they might have built a nest inside the stove. He'd employ a fellow with a ride-on mower to clear the high grass around the house. He could take care of the hands-on stuff. He'd taken one look at the sagging bed bases and dirty pillows and made a note to arrange immediate delivery of new innersprings. The fridge and washing machine were relics from the Second World War era, and would have to be replaced. His main priority now was to arrange boundary fencing. A sizeable creek ran through the property. The agent had looked doubtful but Nathan wasn't concerned about paying the bill. He'd survived the biggest loss a man could imagine and he wasn't about to risk his daughter's safety.

He was looking forward to the clean-up. Shelby had only taken the dog until the weekend. It wouldn't be fair to impose, although she seemed to be an animal lover. An odd girl. At the clinic she'd been confrontational and, at first, definitely unfriendly — then turned around and offered to help him. Perhaps meeting him again, after the rescue on the beach, was hard to deal with. He certainly thought it was uncanny. Rescuing her had been a fortunate start to his new life.

He'd head back into the town later and start ordering the necessary furnishings. Meanwhile, he might as well make a start here. With a satisfying rip, he made a heap of the filthy curtains and systematically shoved up the window frames. Several immediately fell down. He added sash cords to his list. Venturing along the dim hallway, he began to carry the discarded furniture outside.

The bathroom was a shambles. Rusty water spluttered into the ancient bathtub when he tried the taps and the plug was missing. Plug. He'd get some cans of that Rustaway stuff they advertised on TV. At least the old lavatory worked.

One room had newspapers stacked waist-high around the walls. A burn-up in the back yard incinerator would take care of them and the rotted curtains. Who needed privacy in this remote setting? Sunlight slanted along the wooden floorboards. Filthy! Could he hose out the rooms? Might not dry. Mop and bucket.

He'd better add food to his shopping list. He sank down on the dusty velveteen chesterfield to scribble a grocery list, then idly glanced around the room. The radiogram must be half a century old. His parents back in New Zealand still had one like that beside the china cabinet. He'd been lucky to grow up in a home of music, listening to everything from pop music to opera. He knelt down to investigate Bakelite recordings in faded paper cases. Aida! La Traviata! And the performers — Tito Gobbi, Richard Tucker, Maria Callas! Did the old stylus even have a needle? Yes! He set the disc on the turntable and through the hisses and scratches of age rose the timeless music of opera. In neighboring paddocks, cows looked up and dogs barked. As Radames proceeded to the Temple of Vulcan to take up the sacred arms, Nathan's tenor voice joined in the full chorus of Aida's Triumphal March.

* * *

Shelby wrenched the steering wheel, reversing into a driveway and retracing her route back to Maitland. Nathan had implied the house wasn't far out of the town. Since leaving the main street, she'd been driving for ten minutes and there was still no sign of her destination. Had she missed a turnoff? She should have asked him to draw a map.

It was past midday and she was hungry. Nathan hadn't said anything about inviting her to lunch. He probably had his hands full, moving in. Her stomach growled. She ought to have stopped somewhere and bought a snack.

At the back window, Skip was intoxicated by the scenic tour. Presumably he had never been to the country and his wet nose quivered at the smorgasbord of scents as he paced from one side of the back seat to the other, trying Houdini-like maneuvers to escape the car. Shelby had seen too many dogs arrive at the clinic with eye injuries to allow him to stick his head out the window into the fresh air. Intent as she was on searching for the rambling farmhouse resembling Nathan's description, she could only form a general impression of the scenery.

Well-maintained heritage homes lined both sides of the country road running from Maitland through Lorn. Past the small town, cattle and horses grazed lush-looking pasture edged by poplars bare of their leaves in winter. Other low-lying paddocks had a freshly-harrowed neatness, with green shoots setting off the rich brown loam.

She drove through Larg, an even smaller hamlet that she was past before she'd registered its name. This was ridiculous! How could Nathan live out here and commute to work every day? But even as she considered the impractical scheme, something about the peace of this tranquil setting was affecting her. Pulling to the side of the road to consult her road map, she sat inhaling the crisp unpolluted air. Her worries faded. Her unsettled life, the extra workload, near-drowning, even that embarrassing Internet fraud . . . Let it go. She watched a hawk glide overhead on outspread wings. This was just what she needed. Time to drift.

A farmer rattled past in an ancient truck, his friendly wave as measured as his pace.

Shelby narrowed her gaze. Were those beehives in that far paddock? Nathan had mentioned something about a honey farm and stables near the house. She cruised past horses, searching for a driveway. One old house stood well back from the road, lonely in a wilderness of neglected ground. That couldn't possibly be it! Could it? But that was Nathan's vehicle, parked on the grass.

Planks bridged the ditch. Steering cautiously, she edged past leaning gateposts and bumped across rough ground that had been recently mown. Worn-out objects lay scattered about — a bicycle wheel, a broom head, cartons of newspaper, a dog kennel lying on its side. A couple of drab trees leaned against the house windows. How could anyone consider living in such a dump?

A full-on operatic recording was blaring from the open front door. As a powerful soprano voice hit top A, Skip lifted his head, flattened his ears and let out a pained howl. The note resonated and slowly died as Nathan, wearing just a pair of low-slung jeans, appeared at the corner of the house, waving. For perhaps the first time in her life, she was struck by well-proportioned male beauty. From his broad shoulders to his tapering waist, he was an eyeful of muscle, sinew and tanned golden skin. She couldn't help it, damn it, she was ogling the man. He probably knew it because his grin was very confident.

'I'm having a burn-up. Need to supervise, with all the long grass lying around. You go on inside. I'll be there in a jiffy.'

Smoke haze hung in the air. Invisible

insects chirruped steadily. In amateur garden beds fashioned from old tires, self-sown weeds flourished. Rundown as it was, the cottage was really rather picturesque. Peace emanated from paddocks where bees made honey, cows gave milk and horses were agisted.

Skip was whining. He scratched at the window. Keeping him on a firm leash, she let him out. This looked like tick country. She'd remind Nathan to buy him a tick collar. The sagging wire fences would be useless. He would have to build an enclosure; perhaps a running chain meanwhile. Nonetheless, it was a great place for a dog. She tethered him to a post and walked up the three front steps, stepping into a sunlit hallway that had a strangely familiar feeling.

Waiting for Nathan, she wandered around, checking out the rooms. Vivid memories were stirring, of teenage years before she fell ill, when she and Jasmine had dressed in black and sat around dingy rooms with other Goth friends, high on the melodramatic lyrics and mournful cello strings of Gothic rock and punk music. What a contrasting lifestyle to the blandness of her parents' happy marriage and comfortable wealth. She'd learned in a very harsh way that dark lyrics and black nail polish did not even scratch the surface of real violence.

Lost in memories of a time when she'd been a normal adolescent, she was startled when Nathan walked into the kitchen. He smelled sweaty and smoky, very male, and looked beyond attractive with his well-defined pectoral muscles and deep tan. Damn him, why didn't he put on a shirt!

'Thanks for bringing Skip. I need to wash up. Are you hungry? I'm famished. What about making sandwiches?' He indicated a bag of groceries on the bench.

'Have you got any plates? Or knives?'

'Don't think so. Can you improvise? I've got a scalpel in my case.'

She laughed. 'You need to go

shopping. You go and change. I'll see what I can find.'

Searching through drawers and cabinets, she unearthed a few cracked dishes and managed to butter the bread with a spoon handle. Fortunately he'd bought sliced cheese and relish. Not quite gourmet fare, but she couldn't wait to sink her teeth into a substantial snack. She was stacking the sandwiches when Nathan arrived, buttoning a clean if crumpled shirt.

'Let's eat outside. I only have cans of Coke, or iced coffee.'

'Either's fine with me.'

He rummaged in the brand-new fridge. They went to sit companionably on the front steps in the winter sunshine, munching with keen appetites and washing down the food with the refreshing drinks.

'How long have you been a receptionist at the clinic?' He tossed a crust to Skip, who did a mid-air somersault to collect his prize.

'I was a late starter. Before that, I

worked for my father at home. He's a stockbroker. He showed me the ropes of office work.'

'Guess you must be an animal lover?'

'You could say that.' At eight, all she'd wanted was a rabbit. At ten, she had four rats and six white mice. She'd begged her parents for a dog when she was twelve, and spent hours training her Jack Russell until sadly, he was run over. Vet work was the first job she'd felt excited about. Getting that job had felt like a turning point in her life. But that feeling was waning.

Nathan seemed to read her mind. 'You're not so keen on the work?'

'It's just not what I expected. Some of the things you see . . . '

Working with animals had sounded so great. She hadn't made allowances for the fact that sometimes pets were brought in for euthanasia. She had to watch sobbing children and upset parents going through the trauma of parting from a much-loved dog or cat. Then there were the animals who arrived in poor health or grossly overweight. She thought of the tragedies when an owner could not afford the fees to pay for a vet bill, and had to have the animal put down. You simply had to develop an objective view, and not allow yourself to be upset by the incidents that were almost everyday occurrences. So Trevor kept telling her. Could she ever manage that?

'I suppose you always wanted to become a vet?' He seemed the kind of man to know his goals.

'Yes. I grew up with animals. My parents are dairy farmers. They were pleased when I did the five year vet degree at Massey. I think they hoped I'd find work close to home.'

'You're from New Zealand?'

'Yeah. Seems I can't lose the accent! You been there?'

'No. I was planning a trip with my friend, but she's just got engaged and she has other plans now. So why did you move to Australia?'

She'd strayed onto no-go territory.

His manner became withdrawn. He even seemed to physically pull away from her, then abruptly he stood up. 'Long story. Would you like a quick wander round the property? I'll put Skip on a rope until the fences go up.'

Skip on lead, they walked to the back boundary, where a willow-edged creek meandered. Nathan's face was stern as he watched the pup dip a tentative paw in the water.

'How will you stop him wandering?' As far as Shelby could tell, the wires designed to contain horses and cattle would present no challenge to an agile dog.

'I'm having six foot fences erected tomorrow.'

'What, right round the property?' She thought that would cost thousands, but he shrugged.

'I'm paying. I'm not bringing a child here without fences. My wife drowned.'

There it was. A bald statement. It could have been a weather report. His clouded eyes stared into hers, his feelings inaccessible.

'I'd better get on. Thanks for dropping off the dog. I'll catch you later.'

Calling Skip, he left her there and headed back toward the house as though it made no difference to him whether she stayed or went.

* * *

His abrupt change of mood had puzzled her for the rest of the weekend, but she found that at the clinic Nathan was easy to work with. By the end of his first week at the surgery, Shelby noticed a reduction in her workload. Nathan was cooperative, and did not expect her to witness unpleasant medical procedures. Compared to Trevor, he was an easygoing partner, and she wished the head vet would take a leaf from Nathan's book. She would have to take a stand and demand her overdue holiday leave soon. She needed time to find new living arrangements before she could even think of looking around at the job market.

As if reminding her of his authority, Trevor called her in for the extra inventory review he'd mentioned earlier. He left her to hoist cartons and unload high shelves, while he made meticulous counts she couldn't see the point of. Anyone would think he was running a shop. She had to bite back a rebellious impulse to resign. Hardly a smart move. Homeless and unemployed? Not a good look! She simply had to accept the drawbacks of the job.

A few days later, as if to test her further, fate brought an abandoned dog to the clinic. She arrived at work to discover a cardboard box deposited outside the locked surgery. Her nose wrinkled as she peered down at a female Maltese terrier, elderly and very neglected. The smell of her breath and untended coat was awful. Tangles covered her flea-ridden body and fur dangled over her rheumy eyes, almost blinding her. This was exactly the scenario that made Shelby want to give up veterinary work on the spot. As she murmured comforting noises, the homeless dog seemed calm and even affectionate. Attempting to wag her knotted tail, she pressed a dry black nose against Shelby's hand.

'Whatever are we supposed to do with you?' Shelby picked up the envelope tucked in a corner of the box and read the unsigned note.

Grandma has been put into a nursing home. Please find a new home for her dog, Lily.

Lily! Anything less flower-like Shelby couldn't imagine. Her heart was a leaden weight in her chest. Trevor would remind her the surgery was not a charity, and tell her to arrange for the Pound to collect the dog. And, given her age and condition, Lily's fate would be sealed.

She carried the carton inside and placed it on the floor behind the desk. Lily was a sweet little thing, quite uncomplaining as she gazed up at Shelby. A wild idea came to her that she could pay for the animal's veterinary care herself and adopt her. But the timing was all wrong, when she had to move.

She filled a bowl with animal biscuits, but although Lily was hungry her infected teeth and gums made chewing painful. It was pitiful to see her as she tried without success to eat. Giving up, she looked at Shelby as though asking her to help. Outside, a car pulled up in the parking lot. Preparing for another run-in with Trevor, she instinctively stuffed the dog back in the carton and pushed it out of sight behind the counter, but it was Nathan who breezed through the door. Shelby sagged onto the chair facing the computer, pretending to boot up the machine. Nathan gave her a curious look.

'You look upset.'

Wordlessly, Shelby indicated the carton.

Crouching, Nathan peered inside. 'Good grief! Where did she come from?'

'She's been abandoned.' Suddenly the injustice of the world was too much for Shelby's self-control and she swallowed angrily. 'It's so unfair!'

He didn't disagree or offer any of those philosophical thoughts intended to cheer her up.

'Bloody unfair! I know.'

'How can you stand it?'

'What, Shelby?' The kindness she heard in his voice only brought her closer to tears.

'Being a vet. Dealing with all the pain and neglect.'

'Yes, there's plenty of pain and neglect. But there's a lot of joy. Heaps of love. Even the odd miracle!'

She tried to smile. He was right, of course. But that didn't solve the problem with Lily.

Nathan seemed to read her thoughts. 'So what happens with the mutt?'

'I'm supposed to ring the Pound and

see if they're collecting in this area.'

The ever-threatening tears rose again. She somehow identified with the homeless dog that nobody loved or wanted. Lily wasn't to blame because she was diseased and smelly. If it wasn't madness, Shelby would pay the vet fees herself and adopt the little creature.

'I want to keep her.' The words broke from her quivering lips and Nathan seemed concerned.

'Then why don't you?'

'Trevor would object.'

'What's it got to do with Trevor?' He sounded mystified.

'He keeps telling me I'm too involved. We never treat strays. There's no profit.'

Surely Nathan wasn't encouraging her mad impulse to rescue Lily? She remembered he didn't know she had to find a new place to live.

'I don't see the problem. You just need to sort out some arrangement with Trevor. Tell him you want to give Lily a chance, and offer to pay for any meds she needs. I'll do the surgery during my own hours. There'll be dental work for a start.'

Nathan wrinkled his nose and she laughed. He was standing close enough that she could see the grainy texture of a complexion weathered by time and an outdoors life. Laugh lines radiated from hazel eyes that were keenly perceptive as he scanned her downcast face. Suddenly she wanted to hug him.

The forlorn image of Lily being put down was fading. Now Shelby imagined her clean — bathed and clipped, her teeth seen to and her fleas gone. A healthy dog with a new chance at life. Nathan's offer would give her a reprieve.

'Let's get Lily on the table and see just what needs doing. We have half an hour before the patients start arriving.'

Lily had a formidable list of health issues. Her antigen test was fortunately negative, but she needed vaccinations, worm, flea and preventive heartworm treatments. Her ears needed flushing, she had conjunctivitis and extensive tooth and gum disease. Nathan palpated her belly gently and shook his head.

'Her bladder's full of stones. She'll need surgery.' He glanced at Shelby. 'You really want to do this?'

'I'm sure.'

'Okay! Let's talk to Trevor.' He laughed at her reluctance. 'I need you to assist. The guy's not a monster, Shelby. Just state your case.'

And he was right. Trevor simply nodded at Nathan's matter-of-fact account of Lily's problems, and checked with Shelby that she would pay the account. Shelby gave up her lunch hour to run the clippers over Lily's coat and then bathe and flea shampoo her. X-rays confirmed bladder stones and the two vets stayed back after work to carry out the necessary surgery. Intent on the small dog's care, Shelby tried to overcome her anxiety at the sight of the scalpel blade, taking deep breaths and eventually watched with interest. She gasped when she saw the size of the marbled stones Nathan was removing.

'She's probably been in considerable pain. We'll send them off to pathology. Struvite stones, probably. She'll need a prescription diet from now on.'

As Trevor stripped off his overalls and told Shelby to admit Lily for overnight recovery, he even offered a word of praise.

'Well-done. I told you you'd get over the collywobbles in surgery. By the way, I've appointed the new nurse. You can take your holiday as soon as you like.'

The little dog's problems might be dealt with, but Shelby was in shock after she compiled the list of drugs, laboratory fees and surgical procedures she'd agreed to pay for. There was no way she could pay the bill of over a thousand dollars. The clinic had a strict policy of payment at the time of treatment. She was beginning to see that she'd been caught up in a fantasy. She'd always rescued animals. It had seemed natural to save Lily, but she hadn't thought it through. How could she pay that huge bill, and still find money to rent a place with a yard for a dog?

It was Nathan who had a possible solution.

'You could come and stay with me while you sort it out.'

'With you?'

'Caity's arriving any day and I haven't found a suitable woman to help out.'

'I'm not a babysitter! I already have a job.'

'Of course you do. This would be temporary. A few weeks, for starters. I'd pay you, naturally.'

'What makes you think I could take care of your daughter?'

'I've seen the way you are with animals. I know a caring person when I see one.'

She didn't know the first thing about little kids, but was in no position to argue. She had a huge bill to pay. Once again Nathan had come to the rescue. Jason and the others would see she had a good reason to move out.

She passed on her change of plans as soon as she arrived home that evening. Lily would be discharged from the clinic by the weekend. Packing up would be a simple matter, and the boys would soon replace her with one of their mates. Nothing much would change for them.

Jason stood in the doorway of her room as she began sorting her clothes and possessions into piles.

'Where are you moving to?'

'Near Maitland. Country place. Good for Lily.'

'Cool.' He hesitated. 'Guess I'll say goodbye and head out. See ya!'

He made a high-five gesture, offered his lopsided grin and was gone.

Just for a moment, she felt a pang. It was never easy, saying goodbye. Yet the terrifying incident on the beach had taught her life was too precious to waste on resentment or fear of the future. At some stage you had to take responsibility for your life. She knew now she should have listened to that nagging intuition, warning her about tragic begging letters on the Internet. And surely she could have anticipated the frustration of living with a young man who'd barely detached from his mother's apron strings. She did still like Jason, just didn't want to live with him any longer. This time the move felt right. A buzz of excitement filled her while she stuffed the last items in her suitcase and thought of what lay ahead with the new vet. Nathan Monroe and his daughter — which one would be the greater challenge?

4

Nathan's welcome speech wasn't exactly effusive. He stood in the doorway, blocking Shelby's entrance and frowning as he eyed Lily and the heap of luggage Shelby was unloading from her boot.

'I think we should get the ground rules straight.'

He threw in a smile to soften the blunt words, but she realized he must be rethinking his arrangement with her. His authoritarian manner took her by surprise.

'Ground rules? Lights off by ten? No men in the bedrooms?'

The frown re-appeared. 'Look, you do understand this is just a temporary arrangement, until I find a housekeeper? I'm not looking for . . . '

'Neither am I. Are you done with the welcome speech? If so, perhaps you'll let me in. I assume my wing of the palace is that way?'

It wasn't a great beginning.

At least Lily and Skip weren't sparring. Equally pleased to find a friend, the two ill-matched pets ran off to explore the yard. Nathan had obviously kept his word. The dogs were both safely contained now within a formidable chain mesh fence.

Shelby strode past Nathan, carrying her luggage. He'd organized new beds in the three bedrooms. There were singles in the smaller rooms, and a king-size mattress in the room he'd obviously claimed for himself. She'd a good mind to unpack and lay out all her panties and bras on his bed, for a laugh. No, he wouldn't find that funny at all. His stern Mr. Rochester face had given her the impression he wished he'd never agreed that she stay. She ought to remind him it was she who was doing him the favor, not the other way around. She could have stayed with Jasmine, or her parents, for that matter. She could drive away right now, and then who would look after the kid?

No, that was a bad plan. She'd agreed to mind this man's daughter and she couldn't just leave. She wasn't one to go back on her word. And then there was the vet bill. She'd paid it, but all her holiday money was gone.

In the brief time since she'd last been at the house, Nathan had been busy. Paint cans and rollers lined the hallway and he'd given the bathtub a coat of anti-rust. So far, his efforts to spruce up the house only emphasized how much work remained to be done.

He had followed her along the hall and stood in the doorway, watching as she half-heartedly tossed clothing into the drawers of the old tallboy.

'I'm sorry if I sounded rude. I just can't get my head around how I'm going to deal with Caity.'

The uncertain note in his voice puzzled her. It was as though he didn't want to see his daughter.

'What are the arrangements?'

'Barbara is flying down with her from Brisbane.'

'Barbara?'

'Her grandmother. According to her, Caity's not coping. It's only five months since Samantha drowned. Barbara stepped in, because my work tended to take me all over the place.'

'So both her mother and her father disappeared? It's hardly surprising a little girl would be upset.'

'She's more than upset. According to Barbara, she's developed all sorts of behavioral problems.'

'Such as?'

'I don't know. Tantrums, food phobias, whatever unhappy kids resort to . . . '

Nathan was obviously out of his depth. 'I hope I haven't brought you here under false pretenses, Shelby.'

He looked downright miserable, standing there, his fingers twisting his wedding ring. She realized his loss was still raw. His way of coping was denial. He'd simply locked away his pain, shutting out all admission of his anguish. Now a grieving little girl was about to force him to face up to their loss. His defenses were crumbling and she felt terribly sorry for him.

'Hey, we'll deal with it.' She laid a gentle hand on his arm. 'Between us, we'll manage.'

'I hope so,' was all he said.

'If you have visitors arriving, there's work to do. Come on, we'll make a list and work together.'

'Yes, ma'am!' But he looked relieved as he smiled down at her. 'You'd better change that pretty dress. I'll make coffee, then we'll get started.'

Getting the rest of the bedroom walls coated using the roller brushes was straightforward work, but Nathan raised a problem. 'We can't breathe those fumes all night. We'll have to sleep in the lounge room.' He hesitated. 'Is that okay with you?'

'I don't mind camping.' Her light words covered the stab of excitement in her stomach as she thought of sleeping beside Nathan. Quickly she changed the subject. 'Do you mind if Lily sleeps inside? I think she'd feel more secure.' Although it wasn't Lily's welfare that was causing the catch in her breathing and that warm glow deep in her belly as she imagined stretching out on her mattress just an arm's length away from him. It was pure imagination to think there was any more to this interlude than simply helping each other out with a practical problem. Nathan certainly wasn't interested in her. He'd made that very clear even before she'd stepped through the door. His issues were deep and painful, and the arrival of a disturbed child was not going to make life easier.

'Do you want to take the dogs for a walk?' She hoped he'd join her in the late afternoon sunshine, but he stood up briskly.

'You go. I'll clean up and shove a pizza in the oven. Thanks for your help, Shelby.'

He remained distant for the rest of the evening, until she was glad when he shifted the two mattresses and then announced he was going out for a jog. Surely they could have shared the exercise, enjoying the fading light where insects and birds seemed to be claiming the last of the day? She stood in the doorway of the lounge, noting the single mattresses, carefully spaced apart. She was tired after the physical activities of moving house and painting, so what was she waiting for? Nothing was going to happen with Nathan Monroe! Some run! He'd been gone two hours. Skip came back exhausted and flopped down in the yard as though he couldn't face the prospect of climbing three steps.

She was already tucked up under her doona quilt when Nathan came to bed. He spread his own bedding, pulled off his shoes and lay down, fully dressed. The zipper of his sleeping bag had a final sound as he glanced across at her.

'Comfy?'

Actually, the pillow was hard and had a new, rubbery smell. But that wasn't why she was wide awake. A fine, electric energy prickled her skin, sensitizing her. She lay anticipant as the minutes slowly passed. Lily was cuddled by her side.

The paint fumes were noticeable, even here, and the sounds of the night were unfamiliar. A strange bird called, a breeze rattled the windows of the old house, and sharp clicks overhead must be falling twigs, or perhaps a possum walking on the iron roof.

Nathan was only an arm's length away. If she dared, she could reach across and touch his face, and let her fingers explore the crisp, curling hairs on his forearm. She imagined sliding into his sleeping bag and fitting herself along his body, sharing his warmth, basking in his strength. That fine energy charging her senses made her feel their bodies were wired together. She'd never get to sleep unless she could switch off the connection, but how? He obviously didn't feel it. He was as far away from her as that full moon, shining its cold illumination through the uncurtained windows. She heard him sigh.

Her mouth was dry. Could she get a drink of water without disturbing him? Tiptoeing, she went to the kitchen, filled a glass of water and used the bathroom. She wished the paint on the bath was dry. A good hot soak would be so relaxing. Meantime she would simply have to wait out the endless night, and make sure her own room was aired and ready by tomorrow.

* * *

Nathan had watched her summon Skip and Lily and head off toward the creek, her trim figure lost beneath the oversized old T-shirt he'd lent her while she painted. One thing he hadn't bargained on was fancying the babysitter. Nothing had been further from his mind, until she touched him. Her soft little hand on his arm had simply brushed away the barrier that kept all women safely at bay. Her gentle gesture had dismissed his decision to remain immune.

I'm here for you. Talk to me. Let me help.

Without a single word, her touch had

offered comfort and invited him to share his burden.

He'd felt his defenses crack. Damn it, he could have broken down and cried — something he hadn't done, not even on the dreadful day when he received the news of Samantha's accidental drowning. He had to hold his life together, especially now. He'd failed Samantha. If he'd done as she wanted, if he'd taken time off work and gone with her on that visit to see her parents, he might have saved her. The least he could do now was provide Caity with the security and love she deserved; if only he felt better equipped for that task.

He sensed movement and saw Shelby creep past his mattress. He heard a tap run in the kitchen, and now Skip was scratching on the door. He let the dog in and climbed back into the sleeping bag. In a few minutes, Shelby came back to bed. Her slender form outlined in the moonlight was lovely as she quietly eased back under the doona, whispering to Lily. There was a scrabble of little claws on the wooden floor, then silence. The room grew still.

Now he felt alert, as though he was on scout duty while his company rested. His mind began to race with unwelcome images. Samantha was calling to him, unreachable, sucked away by the roaring wall of floodwater. He wasn't there. He didn't know. His wife was gasping, whirling in that torrent, while he was over Gatton way, at Davies' Pig Farm, testing for Circovirus disease. He was eating Mrs. Davies' ginger sponge cake, while Samantha's pleas for rescue went unheeded.

It wasn't his fault. Everyone said that. If not, then whose fault was it? He'd waved them goodbye, Samantha and Caity, never dreaming he would not see his wife alive again. That pallid image in the coffin wasn't her. That was a body, recovered almost a kilometer from where the wall of water snatched her. It wasn't Sam. The real woman haunted his mind. Perhaps she would live there forever, and he would never know peace again.

These night horrors, he couldn't stand them. Usually he did something physical, exhausting, working out with his weights or heading out for a night run. But he'd already tried that, hoping to burn out his memories and give him one night's peace. He had to blame something. The facts alone were just too senseless. His young, beautiful, caring wife, his lover, Caity's mother, was dead. And he was lonely. Bone lonely and yearning for the comfort of her embrace.

The moonlight had shifted and lay across Shelby's face. Her eyes were closed but he sensed she was awake. Her soft lips were parted, her creamy skin glowed in the uncanny light. Soft, her hand had been, that feather touch of sympathy. So soft and small and delicate. What if he stretched across and smoothed back her tumbled fringe of hair? How would they fit, if he slid down beside her, their bodies touching, close and intimate?

What kind of thoughts were those? With an irritable hunch, Nathan turned on his side facing away from her. He huddled lower in his sleeping bag and finally gave in to oblivion.

By morning he was back on terra firma, planning out his day, all impossible fantasies pushed from his mind. Shelby hadn't surfaced when he tossed several fifty dollar notes on the table and scribbled a note, suggesting she could go shopping for whatever she noted was lacking. He scanned the note and added, 'Buy whatever you like.' He had no idea what Caity was likely to eat, given her grandmother's reports. He hoped Shelby would fill in the gaps for him. He had a lot to learn, as a single parent of a disturbed little girl.

Tires spinning on the loose ground, he headed off for work with a spurt of gravel.

* * *

Nathan's hints that Caity was difficult worried Shelby. A troublesome dog she could handle. Affection, discipline and a clear message that she was boss usually got the point across. But she could hardly put Caity in a cage or train her on a leash! How was she supposed to care for a four-year-old? Maybe Jasmine would know. She was a teacher and might have some advice to give.

But when she phoned her friend, Jasmine sounded preoccupied. She and Rob were flying to New Zealand within a week, and she was full of talk about their plans. She hardly seemed to register Shelby's situation.

'Don't worry! You'll figure it out. Keep her amused and establish limits. She'll soon settle down.'

How did Jasmine know that? All she wanted to talk about now was finding somewhere to leave Blade, and Shelby had no intention of adding a horse to her growing responsibilities.

She thought of an alternative. 'We have stables next door. I could find out if they have room for Blade. How long will you be away?'

'Rob's hoping to find work there. If he does, I'll stay.'

Shelby had feared as much. But she bit back the words of disappointment that came to mind. How could she begrudge Jasmine her obvious happiness?

'I'll miss you,' was all she said. 'Shall I ask about boarding?'

'That would be great. You could take Blade for a few rides.'

'I'll check out the costs and ring you back.'

At least she had an excuse now to meet her neighbors. The old house was isolated and strangely silent after the general noise of her previous accommodation. Nathan had told her to make herself at home, but somehow she felt like a visitor. There was still a little time before his daughter arrived. Perhaps he would lose his aloof manner and she'd feel more settled by then. After giving the dogs their morning feed and a few tosses with a tennis ball, she secured them inside the fence and headed toward the old wooden building next door. A pungent aroma of cooking wafted from the door where an elderly Asian man, wrapped in a grey blanket, sat in a wicker chair on the porch, a very pregnant cat in a basket near his feet.

'Are you the owner?'

He must not speak English. He smiled and gestured, indicating she should go inside. Just then a cheerful voice called out, 'Come in!' and Shelby followed the scent of spices to the kitchen.

'I'm Lexi. I've been meaning to welcome you with a small gift.' The petite Asian woman reached up to a shelf lined with jars of honey. 'Please try this. The batch was Manuka blossom.'

'Thanks. Your own product! How do you market it?'

'Oh, we supply local outlets — greengrocer, even the butcher keeps a supply. It's only pocket money. Our main income is from boarding horses.'

'That's what I've come to see you about.' Shelby explained that Jasmine was going overseas and Lexi nodded.

'I keep several old horses nobody else wants. Plus people send me a few for agistment.' She handed Shelby a business card. 'My rates are listed there. Ask your friend to phone me. I can help her arrange transport if she needs a horse trailer.'

'She'll be relieved. She's just got engaged. She's going to New Zealand with her fiancé.'

'Lucky girl!'

Lexi spoke without a trace of envy but Shelby guessed there would be no social life in this isolated setting.

'Are you and your husband settling in?'

'We're not married,' Shelby said, not wanting to go into a string of explanations, and Lexi gave a discreet nod. 'Do you run this place by yourself?'

For it was obvious the old man was

past his working days.

'The house and land belong to my grandfather. His memory's not so good. I keep things going.'

Swiftly she set out cups and biscuits on a tray, as though a visitor must be a rare event.

There was a shrill burble of foreign speech from the porch, and Lexi laughed.

'That's Ông Ngoai, feeling left out! He likes to know everything that's going on.'

She called back in his language, then enlightened Shelby. 'We're Vietnamese. Well, my father was Australian. My mother was from Vietnam. They met during the war. Later, after my grandmother died, my mother brought her father here. She died three years ago, and I follow her wish that I care for her father. It's the custom.'

She was describing a life of sacrifice. Her posture and clothes suggested she wasn't young, though her face was unlined and her hair naturally dark.

What chance would she ever have, living out here, to meet a partner or marry?

Yet there was no trace of resentment in her open smile as she carried the tray outside.

Shelby sat on the weathered porch step, stroking the cat and enjoying the winter sunshine. The unhurried pace of life was such a contrast to her previous days. At the clinic, the phone would be shrilling, clients would come and go and there would be demands and summons to obey. Extending an invitation to her neighbor to return her visit soon, she was thoughtful as she walked home, carrying Lexi's business card and her jar of honey. One friend was moving on. Lexi, with her air of patience and acceptance, might be someone to talk to, and even become a good friend in time.

Elderly horses leaned down to crop, turning their wise fringed eyes to note the stranger passing by. In the distance, Skip was barking and she quickened her pace, pleased to see the two dogs again. Lily stood waiting, her tail whisking like a feather duster. This place offered nothing to boast about but she liked it here. Her parents would be mystified at her choice of accommodation. They spoke as though Shelby should set her sights on the glamor of London, the artistic wonders of Paris. Yet, if Lexi's contentment was genuine, perhaps everything good might be found here, within the boundaries of green paddocks and the rippling creek.

Shelby was thoughtful as she returned to the riotous welcome of the two dogs. They too had the gift of living in the present. Lily did not mourn the loss of her previous owner. Skip's past, whatever it was, did not weigh him down. Harking back to past hurts and mistakes was a human failing. She'd spent enough time brooding. The advice of her parents and her friend had been right, yet second-hand wisdom hadn't really helped.

She felt a slow change, an old injury

dissolving, as though after a cold winter the spring was finally here. Her fingers tingled, her steps were light, until she spun around, laughing, and the dogs joined in, leaping and barking in spontaneous play.

Inside, Shelby wandered from room to room, opening windows to clear the paint smell. She might as well take advantage of Nathan's note. A vacuum cleaner would be handy, the kitchen lacked a few essentials, and a few cushions and throw rugs might brighten up the old furniture. There were no toys or books to interest a child. She'd noted a Book Exchange and Op shop in the town. Perhaps a few hours of retail therapy and lunch at the Vanilla Café would pass the time. Once Caity arrived, she would probably long for peace and quiet.

Making sure the dogs were exercised, she drove toward Maitland, skirting the lazy curves of the Hunter River. Widely-spaced signs along this stretch of road announced boarding kennels and a turf and garden supply business.

The heritage homes leading in to Maitland, and the Gothic lines of the Art Gallery and the church spire, elevated the town despite the mundane presence of Kmart and Woolworths. The unfamiliar feeling that she was a housewife and mother drew her from shop to shop. She chose a colorful animal frieze for Caity's room and selected a pile of children's books at the book exchange, adding an old cookery book from the throw-out bin. Perhaps she could surprise Nathan with something special for dinner.

In the Op shop, she quickly passed over winter cardigans and skirts, then found she was searching the racks for children's clothes and even menswear. That olive sweater would bring out the green flecks in Nathan's hazel eyes . . . Stop! She turned and hurried out of the shop. Her bad experience as a teenager had turned her off men for life, she'd believed. Nathan might be the first man she'd felt attracted to in years. She'd go so far as to say that in some parallel universe she'd found her soul mate. But that was pure fantasy. Nathan saw her as a nanny. Shelby Summers was here to do a job. He might be interested in any preparations she was making for Caity's arrival. That was all.

What did she know about Nathan? Virtually nothing. His life as a husband and father was a closed book. He had a breadth of life experience that made her feel like a novice. She'd never had a serious relationship, never held a baby in her arms, never known deep love or suffered the cruel pain of loss he'd been through. Would he open up and talk to her as time passed? At least they wouldn't have to share adjacent beds tonight. The undercurrents of the previous night had left her with an odd, unsettled sense of intimacy — as though, despite the boundaries he'd been so quick to put in place, there was an unspoken attraction between them.

But he could switch moods in a flash, erecting an emotional distance around him that was as impenetrable as any material wall. As she drove back to the house, she hoped her unsettled feeling would pass. She and Nathan needed to form an adult understanding before a child was added to the household.

No doubt he felt the same. Over the coming days as they waited for Caity's arrival, he cheerfully moved furniture, struggled to hang the frieze, and walked the dogs with Shelby. She heard him singing a few times, and enjoyed his mellow tenor voice. He introduced her to opera, inviting her to listen to scratched recordings of La Bohème and La Traviata. A few times her eyes filled with tears at the sheer beauty of the arias, and she'd feel his gaze, almost as though he was seeing something in her that intrigued him. But that was wishful thinking.

Just as easily, he could switch off. He would sit, silent and withdrawn, avoiding her presence, staring at nothing. If she tried to talk him out of his mood, he would pull on his joggers and take off on one of his arduous runs, leaving her feeling abandoned.

'Barbara's arriving with Caity tomorrow,' he announced one evening.

'You must be excited?' She hoped her own reaction of dismay was temporary. It was hard enough adjusting to Nathan, without throwing a disturbed child into the mix. How on earth was she going to cope, here alone all day while he went off to the clinic?

'Is there anything I need to do before they get here?' she offered.

'Not really. Barbara can use my bedroom and I'll sleep on the couch.'

'How long will she be staying?' Perhaps his mother-in-law could spend a few weeks helping Caity settle in to a new caretaker.

'Only a couple of days.'

That was that. He did not sound particularly happy that his little girl was arriving.

Did he have any idea how apprehensive she was?

'Do you want me to come out to the

airport to meet them?'

He gave an indifferent shrug. 'No need. I'll drive out after work.' He seemed to be saying her presence was immaterial. She had to remember this was simply a short-term job. The companionship they'd begun to share was in her imagination. Naturally he would transfer his time and attention to his family. What would she say if Caity's grandmother grilled her on her experience with children? Would it seem strange if his visitors found a young woman already in possession of the house? Better that she gave them some time to themselves.

'I was planning to visit my parents tomorrow,' she improvised, trying to gauge his reaction. He obviously didn't care if she wasn't at home to welcome Caity, judging by his abrupt acknowledgment. Well, two could play that game. As soon as he headed out for one of his solitary runs, she phoned her mother and arranged to drive home for lunch the next day.

5

Leaving the dogs secure with their bones and water bowls, Shelby backed out of the drive and headed to the Central Coast turn-off. Her father, Andrew Summers, worked from home as a successful stockbroker based in a beautiful lakeside property halfway between Sydney and Newcastle. Shirley, her mother, had given up paid office work to follow her dream of writing a novel. Andrew, shifting his considerable intelligence to e-book marketing, had helped her design a website and cover, and Shirley's first crime thriller was already selling on the Internet.

Shelby's childhood had been both affluent and loving, and somehow she felt her parents deserved a more successful daughter. They'd supported her through her teenage illness. She felt that was enough, surely, for any parents to deal with. They knew nothing about last year's Internet scam she'd fallen for or her recent panic attack after the frightening near-drowning that still haunted her dreams.

Failure just wasn't a concept in their contented, productive lives. Neither Andrew nor Shirley showed any signs of physical decline. Attractive and physically fit, on their daily walks they reminded onlookers of those happy older couples on brochures advertising successful retirement plans. Andrew maintained a full client list, while Shirley's outlines of future novels would keep her busy for the next twenty years. Shelby wondered what their latest news was. On the phone, her mother had hinted she had an important piece of news to share.

As Shelby pulled up on their circular driveway, ringed by manicured gardens and a tasteful water feature, she wondered what her parents would think of her present accommodation. Opting to live in Nathan's old house would be beyond their comprehension, though they would tactfully say nothing, saving their reactions for each other. The rental house was a temporary step for Nathan and his daughter, but even explaining that would introduce a note of tragedy that so far seemed to have eluded Shirley and her handsome husband. His iron-grey hair was sleek and his olive complexion barely lined. There he was, stepping out of the panelled front door now, his welcoming smile loving as he held out his arms in a gesture of affection.

'Come in, sweetheart! Mum's just gone to the shops to pick up a snack for lunch.'

'Hi, Daddy!' Close in his embrace, she felt the years drop away. His warm hug exuded safety, security, love — the perfect ingredients a child needed. Except that she was no longer a child, in need of fatherly protection and advice. Andrew was taking his time understanding his daughter had grown up.

He'd trained her in office work and was disappointed when she found the independence to leave home. Last time she'd visited, she'd mentioned casual plans to backpack in Europe with Jasmine, and had regretted it as soon as Andrew pointed out the risks of terrorism, the euro crisis and the civil uprisings and demonstrations so regularly aired on television.

'I'm an adult now,' she'd reminded him, but he'd shaken his head as if to say she would always be his little girl.

'Your Mum rang the clinic. They said you were on leave. Why not come and stay with us?'

'It was all rather last minute. And I'm helping mind a friend's little girl.'

'Still collecting waifs and strays?'

He spoke fondly, but the implication that she was gullible jarred. She didn't think of Nathan and his daughter as pitiable. Life had delivered them an exceptionally cruel blow they had in no way earned, and if she could help, she would.

'Come and see my latest project.' Andrew led the way through the large foyer with its potted fernery and huge birdcage of doves. His study reminded Shelby of a dance floor, its parquet floor scattered with luxurious rugs and the latest in computer technology arrayed on a massive antique desk he'd acquired at auction and had transported from Melbourne. Shelby eyed an expensive-looking classical guitar, propped on its stand.

'Who's learning the guitar?'

'Just a little hobby I've taken up. Never had time for music till now. Something to entertain me in my old age.' He laughed incredulously, as though such a state could never happen to him. 'I try and put in two or three hours every day, while your mother's writing.'

'Good one!' Shelby concealed a smile. Since when did her father ever do anything in a half-hearted manner? Two or three hours a day did not sound like a little hobby.

She wandered to stand at the floor-to-ceiling picture window. The grey expanse of the lake lay just a hundred meters from the house, where the background bush was a soft smudge of olive on the opposite shore. A flotilla of black swans, a hundred or more, flowed in pairs across the gleaming surface.

Her father's gaze followed their graceful passage. 'It's unusual for them to gather at this time of day.'

'Perhaps they're migrating?' Shelby wasn't familiar with the habits of swans but Andrew quickly corrected her.

'Swans don't migrate but they're nomadic. They follow food sources. There must be plenty of aquatic plants out there.'

Used to her father's encyclopaedic knowledge, Shelby half-listened, leaning against him. She smiled as a flight of comical ducks landed, fluttering their wings and waggling their tail feathers. Closer to the house, a flock of crested pigeons pecked busily on the grass. Just then her mother's BMW turned into the driveway and pulled up behind Shelby's Yaris, a twenty-first birthday present from her parents. Red-haired and energetic, Shirley bounced out of her vehicle like a teenager, presenting a trim rear view as she leaned into the hatch to unload her shopping. Andrew watched, his expression doting.

'Mum looks happy.'

'Yes. Writing has given her a new direction. She'll tell you about it.'

Her parents reminded Shelby of those paired swans, needing nobody else to complete their happiness. She was lucky to have such role models. Except that she felt excluded. She was looking at love, and being reminded she was alone. She longed to say to her father, 'How did you ever find each other?' But he would only smile and make a joke, not understanding why she would ask him such a question.

Shirley's snack lunch consisted of gourmet salads, cold meats and imported cheeses, washed down with sparkling grape juice and good coffee. She kept pressing Shelby to eat, as though feeding an invalid. It was an old habit from teenage days; irritating concern. Shelby changed the subject.

'You said you have news, Mum?'

'Her mother's blue eyes sparkled. 'I do! I've had a nibble from a British agent who's looking for my type of book. She checked out my website and wants to know if there's a sequel to Dead Lucky. Did you read the copy I gave you?'

'Not yet.' What else could Shelby say? Her mother, an admirer of the Swedish crime thriller author, Stieg Larsson, might not understand sadistic descriptions of tortured victims and rivers of blood repulsed her sensitive daughter.

'This is my big chance. Never walk away from an open door! I'm already halfway through Death Wish. So Daddy and I are going to visit the UK and combine a holiday with seeing this agent. There's nothing like the personal touch.'

'Sounds fabulous! When are you leaving?'

'We'll catch the end of the English summer. That's what we want to talk to you about. Shelby, we'd like to give you a trip.'

'You mean, go with you?'

'You've been talking about that back-packing holiday with Jasmine. Frankly, darling, we're just a little worried. One hears such gruesome stories. I mean, tramping around foreign countries . . . '

'Mum, I'm twenty-two!'

Her parents meant well. An overseas holiday was a brilliant offer, yet travelling with her parents wasn't exactly what she'd had in mind. She felt backed into a corner. Did they think she was incapable of managing without their protection?

'I'd have to think about it.'

'Of course. Your job. Couldn't you take time off?'

'I have a lot going on at present.' Her job. Not to mention Lily and Nathan and Caity and a string of unknowables already feeling like responsibilities.

As she drove back to Maitland, she felt apprehensive, wondering exactly what was waiting for her.

* * *

Nathan was hot on the heels of the exuberant dogs as she pulled into the drive-way.

'Shelby! I was beginning to wonder where you were!'

Nathan sounded more than relieved to see her. Did he really think that, without a word, she would opt out of their agreement?

'Mum and Dad took me for a drive. They wanted to show me a piece of investment real estate they've just bought at Gosford.'

'Come and meet Barbara.'

A pleasant-faced woman in her fifties looked up from the chesterfield at Nathan's introduction.

'You're the nanny who'll be looking after Caity?'

Her tone was friendly. Well-groomed

in a tailored suit and heels, she was a slim, attractive figure, though her strained expression reflected the losses she'd suffered.

'I'll be helping out for a short while with Caity, yes.'

Shelby braced herself for an onslaught of questions as to her relationship with Nathan and her suitability as a nanny, but Barbara was evidently only too relieved to hand over her granddaughter.

'It's time she had a stable home with her father.'

'That's why I've given up rural work,' Nathan reminded her.

'And of course you'll be buying a suitable home, Nathan?' Barbara was obviously not impressed by the shabby premises he'd rented.

'I want to look around for a while before I do that. Selling my land may take months. I might move out of vet work altogether and work from home. Something with animals; there are a few smallholdings in the area.'

Listening to the conversation, Shelby

felt sidelined. Nathan clearly had plans he hadn't felt concerned her. She was a stopgap measure, until his real life resumed. She spoke abruptly.

'Where's Caity?' If she was just the nanny, she might as well meet her other half. Wherever she was, she wasn't making a sound, and the house was peaceful.

'She's eating in the kitchen.'

'I'll go and say hello.'

Nathan led the way to a little girl wearing a pink tracksuit and an adult-sized Akubra hat perched on her ears. She glanced up from the floor where she was seated, spooning strawberry yoghurt into the dogs' dishes. Shelby dropped to eye level and smiled.

'Hi, Caity, I'm Shelby. The dogs shouldn't have your yogurt. That's for you.'

'No-o-o-o.'

Nathan murmured, 'Apparently she only eats banana flavored yogurt.'

He sounded out of his depth. It wasn't the right time to lay down rules.

'Okay! I'll go to the shops tomorrow. Well, Caity, it looks like you're going to be hungry tonight . . . unless you like cheese sandwiches?'

'No-o-o-o.'

'And of course you don't want pancakes with raspberry jam?'

'No-o-o-o.'

'Not even if you stir the batter?'

Caity dripped the last of the yogurt into Skip's bowl.

'Let's not waste that. You bring that bowl, and we'll give Lily and Skip a treat outside.' At least the dogs would be happy. Caity picked up the dishes and a grubby T-shirt she apparently treasured. Outside, she watched the pets eat, an expression of satisfaction on her face. She was a beautiful child, lithe and slender, her rosy cheeks tanned from the Queensland sunshine. Under the oversized hat, a tangle of dark curls straggled to her shoulder blades.

Tenderly, she touched Lily's scar, her dark eyes enquiring as she glanced up at Shelby.

'She was sick. Your daddy fixed her. He's a very clever vet.'

Caity nodded. 'Why was she sick?'

'Her owner didn't look after her properly. Her coat was all knotty, and she had stones in her tummy.'

'Poor Lily.'

Shelby noted the gentle way she stroked the old dog before she stood up, stumbling a little, her yawn shaded by the hat brim.

'Time for bed?'

Shelby waited for a No-o-o-o. Caity just yawned again. Shelby picked her up and turned to Nathan, who had been watching the interplay from the step.

'How about Daddy tucks you up in bed?'

As Nathan reached out to take his daughter, just for a moment they were a trio of closely intertwined arms and hands. Pausing on the top step, he mouthed, 'Thanks.' Just the one word, but it made her feel they were a team, reclaiming a child who was troubled.

Leaving Nathan to put Caity to bed,

Shelby joined Barbara, who had taken note of the interaction.

'You've a way with children,' she confirmed.

Shelby was careful not to explain just how little experience she really had, for Barbara must surely be anxious, leaving her granddaughter with a stranger.

'I suppose we could have run Caity a warm bath to relax her,' Shelby suggested, but Barbara's expression said otherwise.

'I'm afraid you'll have a fight on your hands on bath days. Since the accident, Caity avoids water.'

'Then how do you keep her clean?'

'With great difficulty! Sponge baths, mainly. She hasn't let me wash her hair for a month.'

So that explained the knots in that profusion of curly hair. 'Shelby, I've done my best but I'm starting to think Caity may need professional care. A child psychiatrist, and medication . . . '

'Let's wait and see.' It seemed a drastic solution, and surely being returned to her father would be a major step in the right direction.

Nathan was gone for ten minutes, and when he returned he seemed puzzled.

'That was odd. Caity insisted on looking in all the bedrooms, pulling back the covers, and she asked me if this was a better place. I said, 'Better than what?' and she said she didn't know.'

Barbara spoke defensively. 'That's because I said her mother was asleep and she'd gone to a better place. I meant it to comfort her, but now she goes through this ritual all the time. Poor little thing.'

'Death's pretty hard to deal with, much less explain to a four-year-old.' Shelby's voice was sympathetic, as she thought of her own sadness for the many pets that had made their final journey through the clinic doors.

'True.' Barbara sounded choked. 'One minute we were driving off to Brisbane for a day of shopping. The next, my daughter and my husband were both gone. No time to even say goodbye. I'll never get over it.'

'You've done a tremendous job,' Nathan reminded her. 'And they say life goes on.'

'Yes. They do say so.' But she and Nathan shared a glance that said they didn't believe a word of it.

* * *

Skip's barking woke Shelby early, and she wandered down the hall, remembering Nathan had said he would be leaving early to perform a hysterectomy at the clinic. As she tidied his sleeping bag and pillows, Barbara joined her, yawning. Somehow the homely action made her seem more approachable. She looked so drawn that Shelby was concerned.

'Didn't you sleep well, Barbara?'

'On and off. The bed was very comfortable but a tree branch kept scratching on the window. I'm sorry if you had to move into the spare room on my account.'

She was fishing. For some reason, Shelby blushed.

'There's nothing like that between Nathan and me.'

'It's not my business!' Barbara's tone became confidential. 'To tell you the truth, I'd be happy to hear he was moving on. Prolonged grief's a waste. Believe me, I've learned that. When Bruce and Samantha were taken, I didn't think I could face life without them. The pain was terrible. And in a way it still is. But I've realized I must value the gift I have, of living my own life. I don't know why I was spared. It's my duty to find out.'

Here was a complete stranger, talking from the heart, confiding, sharing. The contrast with Nathan was so marked that Shelby could not let it pass.

'I can't imagine what you and Nathan have been through. I just know he hasn't reached your level of acceptance.'

'He hasn't talked about Samantha at all?' In response to the shake of Shelby's head, she sighed. 'I'm afraid she'll always hold first place in Nathan's heart. You see, they were so much in love. He followed her from New Zealand, you know. And they had Caity to raise.'

With the concern of a wife and mother, Barbara sat gazing into the past.

'No matter how much I miss Bruce, I do know we shared over thirty wonderful years together. Loss is never over, Shelby. It's something we carry with us and perhaps we're kinder, knowing what other people go through.'

Her words were interrupted as Caity, in pajamas and Akubra, arrived in search of Lily.

Barbara gave the protesting child a sponge bath, brushed her teeth and dressed her in clean clothes, then agreed to accept tea and toast. She was booked to fly home the following day. Before that, she offered to make a shopping list of Caity's food preferences and other needs.

'We'll take a run into Maitland later,' Shelby suggested. She was determined to learn more about Samantha's drowning before she was left to cope alone with a grieving child and a silent father.

Her opportunity occurred at lunch-time, when their shopping was done and Caity had finished her kid's meal at McDonald's. As the little girl ran off to explore the indoor playground, Barbara glanced around, her expression mystified.

'Do you know, I'd never set foot in a place like this until recently. I was desperate to find something Caity would eat. Oh, she has been a handful! I hope her father can instill some discipline.'

She sighed, smoothing her cyclone-proof hairstyle and dabbing her mouth daintily with a paper serviette. Her well-bred mannerisms were quite unconscious, but made Shelby feel she was eating too fast. She set aside her hamburger and chose words that would not seem too inquisitive.

'I've only known Nathan a few

weeks. He's never told me about Samantha, or how she died.'

Barbara was only too pleased to talk about her daughter.

'Oh, everybody loved Sam,' she said. 'She knew how to behave, was always ready to help the community. After those first floods, when so many homes and businesses were inundated with mud and silt, she was in there, helping clean up.'

Shelby nodded. She'd seen the downpour and its aftermath on television. Many areas had been declared disaster zones. Roads became rivers, and paddocks were lakes where disoriented cattle stood forlornly packed on any solid ground they could find. There were numerous losses of livestock and vehicles, and stranded families took refuge on roofs or climbed trees. Even so, several human lives were claimed.

Slowly Barbara scraped the food scraps onto a plate and pushed the tray aside, leaning toward Shelby as though wanting to keep the story private.

'I've never really understood Nathan's values, you know. He's such a casual man. Look at that old car he drives. And that rental house! You'd never think he was a wealthy man.'

'I didn't know he was.' Thinking of her own well-off parents, who occasionally conveyed similar attitudes to her, Shelby felt an urge to defend Nathan. 'Some people don't want to be bothered with the trappings of money.'

Barbara was genuinely surprised. 'I don't see why not. I'm sure Samantha did! Oh, perhaps not when they first married. She broke my heart, turning down a proper wedding with all the trimmings. Said Nathan didn't want a fuss. Imagine! Some of our relatives have never forgiven me. As if it was my fault!'

Barbara was evidently a kind woman, but very sure where proper behavior lay as she waved to Caity through the plate glass partition.

'But after several years with Nathan, I know Samantha wanted a nice big house, not some ranch in the back of beyond.' She leaned toward Shelby, lowering her voice. 'She wanted a proper social life. There was tension, she admitted as much to me. My husband was having tests on his heart function and she was worried. She said she was glad of an excuse to get away and visit us. I gathered things were serious.'

'I guess all married couples disagree.'

'I can only tell you she arrived with enough luggage to last a long time. Bruce, my husband, made a joke of it, asked if she was moving back home. She didn't deny it. She seemed depressed. I was worried, naturally.'

There was a catch in her voice. 'I tried to talk to her but Samantha was always stubborn. I suggested marriage counseling. She was in a strange state of mind and Caity was bored. Well, Bruce and I decided to drive them to Brisbane and give them a day out. Shopping, lunch, and a look around town . . . you know. Caity was so excited. It was raining, but we'd had plenty of that for weeks. There was nothing out of the ordinary in the weather forecast.'

She paused, and Shelby saw the tears welling in her eyes.

'We had no idea that water was building into a flash flood. It came out of nowhere, straight at us. We were trying to get the doors open. The car suddenly aquaplaned and started tipping. Water was over the bonnet. Bruce yelled at us to get out. We were being washed over the embankment. Sam had Caity. Somehow we managed to get through the rushing water and scramble up the bank. I nearly didn't make it. That's when Sam realized Bruce was trapped in the car.'

Her face was a mask of disbelief. Shelby reached across the table and took her thin hand.

'She thrust Caity at me and said she was going back for her father. The water simply swept them both away. I could only stand and watch. What could I do? I had to save Caity so I went to beg shelter in a nearby house that stood above the level of the water.'

'And Nathan wasn't even there?'

'No. He came immediately. There was nothing any of us could do except identify the bodies and arrange the funerals. Oh, Nathan tried shuffling Caity between him and me, but his work covered too wide an area. It was best that I keep Caity for a few months while he made arrangements for their future.'

Barbara leaned back, exhausted. 'I've done my best. I'm only sorry she's not the sunny little girl she was six months ago. I hope it won't be too much for you, Shelby.'

'We'll manage. Can I ask you something? What's with the hat?'

'Her mother's. It's the same with that rag of a shirt she carries around. She's inconsolable if it gets mislaid.'

Together they watched the small girl tackle the climbing frame, where she swung upside down, the cumbersome hat dangling by its chinstrap. She waved, delighted to show off, and any doubts Shelby felt faded. That thick brown hair with its chestnut lights was so like her father's; but surely she must have inherited her mother's eyes, for there was no trace of Nathan's green and golden tints in their chocolate depths.

'Caity and I will get along just fine,' she said, and Barbara offered a relieved smile.

* * *

Barbara flew home the following day. As Nathan was at work, Shelby drove her to the airport. While Barbara went to confirm her ticket and check her baggage at the counter, Shelby stood enjoying the busy atmosphere of people in transit. Jasmine was also due to fly out shortly; the transfer of Blade to Lexi's property was complete. Shelby's parents would likewise soon be headed to the other side of the world. If she accepted their offer, she could be one of these focused travelers, heading to new horizons. The jets now slowly circling on the tarmac were tempting symbols of adventure and freedom. She imagined walking into the departure lounge and obeying the call to board her plane. She would meet new people, see new places. She only had to choose.

There wasn't time to wonder now. Caity, charged up with the surrounding energy, was racing from one end of the airport lounge to the other. Shelby retrieved her, bought her an ice cream cone and found a table in the food court. You couldn't take your eyes off a small child for a moment. How did real mothers manage? Barbara was coming toward them now, the look on her face showing she was relieved to be going home. As her flight was announced, she bent and kissed her granddaughter. Caity was preoccupied; the ice cream was melting. Drips ran all over her fingers and, as Shelby reached for paper serviettes, the melting cone cascaded into Caity's lap. Apart from the sticky mess on her face, hands and clothes, her fingernails were grimy and her hair looked unkempt. Shelby made up her mind. This child had to have a bath, and soon.

'Let's go home,' she suggested, once Barbara was out of sight through the turnstiles.

There was no sign of a tantrum. Caity did not ask where her grandmother was. The child was simply swept along by the tide of adults coming and going for their own mysterious reasons. Back at the house, Shelby decided to use psychology in order to overcome Caity's water phobia. While it was completely natural for the child to dread the power of the force that had taken her mother, something had to be done.

'I think it's time we groomed the dogs. Want to help? The brush is in the drawer.'

Delighted to participate, Caity fetched the brush and comb. Suspecting trouble, Skip made a judicious exit, while Lily came compliantly in answer to Caity's summons.

'Why hasn't she got proper hair like Skip?'

'Her owner didn't bathe her or look after her coat. The vet had to cut off her knots and shave all her hair.'

'I've got knots. Will my hair be shaved off?'

'I hope not. I know what we can do! Let's run a bath and shampoo your hair, and you can show Lily it doesn't hurt. I'll get clean towels.'

She left the little girl chatting to the dog. As she returned, she overheard the one-sided lecture. Caity was clearly repeating some past encounter with her frustrated grandmother.

'Lily, this simply has to stop. What will people think if you go about unwashed? Listen to me, young lady! You are going to have a bath whether you like it or not.'

Her strict tone captured Barbara's voice so well that Shelby had to stifle her laughter.

Caity had hoisted Lily onto the bathroom stool, where the white dog sat, her head tipped to one side as though paying careful attention to Caity's tirade. She remained there while a very grubby child had a serious encounter with soap, shampoo and talcum powder. Dry and wrapped in a big towel, she beamed at the obliging dog. 'See, it's easy!'

Lily wagged her tail. She recognized approval and did not need to know she'd played her own small part in helping Caity with her phobia. It was Lily's turn to be bathed, but Skip remained in hiding despite persuasive calls and rattles of the dog treat tin.

'Perhaps we'll do him tomorrow,' suggested Shelby. She was more interested in removing the knots and tangles from Caity's curls. Expecting a battle, she was relieved that the child seemed accepting. After using the hairdryer and brush, Shelby turned Caity to the mirror.

'There! Isn't that better? You're lucky

to have such pretty curls. My hair's dead straight.'

'My mummy had curls. I used to brush her hair sometimes.'

Caity considered her reflection, her dark eyes intent. Her serious expression showed a glimmer of the beautiful woman she would become. Undoubtedly she had inherited her coloring and feminine attributes from Samantha.

A lump formed in Shelby's throat as she thought of all the mother and daughter moments Caity had lost. The figure who should have been there to listen, advise, and comfort was gone — swept away to some 'better place.' How could any child believe that was desirable? Mourning would be a long process.

Yet Caity had the resilience of childhood. By the time she was dressed she had forgotten about farewelling her grandmother and having the bath. With a giggle, she snatched up the tin of talcum powder and raced outside in search of Skip. Watching from the door,

Shelby saw the elusive animal emerge from behind the shed, Caity in pursuit. Shelby grinned when he shook himself in disgust, releasing the snowstorm Caity had showered him with.

The little girl was laughing. Could patience and love heal the losses of her young life? If only Nathan was as responsive! He was so changeable, sometimes turning and walking away abruptly as though there was something about Shelby he disliked.

Barbara's words kept repeating in Shelby's mind.

Samantha will always hold first place in Nathan's heart.

6

Nathan headed into the homebound traffic, his expression somber and his grip on the wheel aggressive. Something fishy was going on at the clinic. A new receptionist had turned up and had even taken over Shelby's puppy classes. The odd events Shelby had mentioned — an extra inventory and Trevor's sudden keenness for her to take her holidays — slotted into place when he overheard Trevor on the phone. Unless Nathan was mistaken, it sounded as though a merger for the clinic was underway. Surely Trevor would have warned him, before offering him the job? He'd attributed Shelby's dislike of the head vet to a simple personality clash, but only a devious man would appoint staff without telling them the facts. If new owners preferred to bring their own staff with them, his position could be in doubt. He'd never wanted to take a city job, but at least Caity was with him now, and the last thing she needed was another move.

His mother-in-law had been great, stepping in to help, but she had her own sorrow to deal with. Even Samantha had agreed her mom was a fusser. Perhaps she'd overreacted to Caity's behavior? How was he supposed to be mother and father when he'd never had any training? Even finding a full-time caretaker was impossible. His inquiries just kept running into blank walls. What was he supposed to do once Shelby's holidays ran out and she returned to work — if she still had a job to go to?

Frustrated, he honked the horn at the slow driver ahead. Hell, what he'd give to be driving through the outback now, with 'roos bounding across the paddocks, emus striding away as he roared past in a blur of red dust. The large-scale breeding programs and splendid pedigreed animals of country veterinary work were in his blood. His parents were farmers. He didn't mind small animals but doting owners of spoiled pets stuck in his gullet. All those years of training he'd put in, only to be stuck now in a tiny consulting room, administering vaccinations, checking flea allergies, or trying to eke out a few more months of life for some cancer-ridden old dog who'd rather be peacefully buried under a gum tree . . .

City people might think country folk were pragmatic, the way they bred and worked their animals, but at least they didn't dress them in Santa suits at Christmas time. Working animals were commodities in the economic cycle, but they earned respect for their intelligence and skill. Even love. He'd seen more than one rugged old farmer wipe away a surreptitious tear when the time came to part.

And as he swung sharply onto the Maitland turnoff, thinking of home and Shelby, an involuntary stirring reminded him he had more on his mind than work. He must have been crazy, letting that girl into his life. The first time he'd seen her asleep after her rescue, he'd had the good sense to turn and run. The memory was imprinted on his mind. Her soft skin, her parted lips, that half-revealed breast rising and falling lightly as she slept . . . And now she was living with him, day and night. Mainly night. He simply hadn't thought it through. Maybe he didn't want to remember he was a single man now. The love of his life was gone, and after six months his basic male drives were wide awake and giving him a sharp nudge.

Was she stirring him up deliberately? She wandered around in her pajamas and what about the way she emerged from the steamy bathroom, draped in nothing but perfume and a towel?

Last night, if she'd known what he was thinking when she bent down to pull that sausage-in-batter thing out of the oven, she wouldn't keep wearing those hip-hugging jeans. He'd stood behind her, stock still, staring at the sweet curves of her luscious behind and feeling his greedy hands itch to grab her and tug down her zipper . . .

Don't go down that road! He had to concentrate all his attention on Caity, and remember that Shelby was the babysitter. At least he could keep to himself in his bedroom. Once Caity was tucked up, he could shut his door and catch up on that pile of journal articles. In a few weeks, he'd find a replacement, she'd be gone and out of his hair.

Although, if a clinic merger was really in the offing, her job might be as insecure as his own. How was it possible that a few weeks ago he'd believed he was making a fresh start? He'd driven this road, telling himself things were actually going to work out. Now it was very clear to him that, whatever external changes he made — changing his job, his living arrangements, perhaps even his partner — it would make no difference. As far as he was concerned, his life had ended the day the flood waters had taken Samantha.

* * *

Shelby glanced at her watch, although she didn't really need to check the time. Her internal clock knew that any minute now Nathan would arrive and pull up in a spurt of clay and dust. The dogs would dash out to greet him but she would wait inside, pretending she was busy in the kitchen.

He wasn't coming home to her and he wouldn't be glad to see her. She'd hoped that, once Barbara went home, Nathan would relax and they could work as a team with Caity.

She was discovering the role of nanny overlapped with half a dozen other jobs she hadn't thought about. Sometimes, Caity was amenable, standing on a chair to stir red jelly or pressing raisin faces into scone dough. The tattered cookbook turned out to be a treasure trove of old-fashioned recipes. Caity sat turning the pages, considering quaintly-named dishes like Toad-in-the-Hole, Devilled Sausages or Patty Cakes. The work involved with cooking, laundry, grocery shopping and housework left Shelby weary and wondering how mothers ever had a moment to themselves. Perhaps if you were living with a man you loved, and who loved you . . .

But Nathan seemed to grow more distant by the day. Even cold. Last night while they sat waiting for the news on TV she'd tried to tell him about Caity's scene in the supermarket.

'She just lay down in the aisle, screaming, and refused to get up. People were avoiding me as though I was a child abuser. When I tried to pick her up, one old woman came up to me and said, 'Don't give in to her. You're making a rod for your own back.''

Nathan shrugged. 'If it's too hard for you, just say. I've made inquiries for your replacement.'

His words were an insult and she flushed. 'I didn't say it was too hard. It's not about me. Caity isn't coping.'

He obviously thought she was exaggerating, but after days of dealing with

Caity's phobias and tears, Shelby was beginning to think Barbara might be right. It was time to consult a professional. Nathan clearly didn't want to know about his daughter's problems. Shelby changed the subject.

'How was your day at the clinic? Anything interesting?'

He just brushed her off as though he couldn't be bothered talking, and viewed the low pressure system indicated on the weather map. The presenter was issuing a cyclone warning for several coastal towns in Queensland, while footage of the January floods filled a short segment before the evening news. Nathan stared at images of people stranded on rooftops or clutching tree branches, while livestock stood thigh-deep in the swirling waters. Buried roads were dotted with abandoned vehicles, some afloat, others lying at crazy angles where they'd been washed up. With a grim expression he stood up and turned the television off.

'Why don't we take Caity and the

dogs for a quick walk?' Shelby suggested, wanting to distract him.

'It's a bit late,' was all he'd said. Once Caity was tucked in for the night, he shut himself away in his bedroom. He hadn't even bothered to say goodnight.

How had she ever imagined he had any interest in her, apart from her role as a nanny?

Like it or not, there were issues they had to sit down and discuss — the most pressing being a suitable full-time nanny. That thought caused a lurch in her heart. The little girl had been through so many losses and changes. Soon she would have to start all over again, learning to trust another stranger. What if the woman Nathan chose did not understand Caity's needs? Everyone had some theory on childcare. Shelby was no expert, but already she felt affection for the little girl and wanted to help her get over her problems. It seemed such a shame to interrupt her progress but there was no choice.

As she drifted off to sleep, she came

to a decision. She'd come to this house as a visitor, accepting a favor from a man who she'd built up in her mind as an ideal. But Nathan was just a screwed-up man with problems of his own. And Shelby was going to remind him it was Caity who mattered now. First thing in the morning she intended to lay it on the line with Nathan. He needed to get over his misery and think of his daughter. Feeling resolute, she fell asleep.

But Nathan was gone by the time she woke next morning. A glance outside showed the storm clouds from further north were starting to move down into New South Wales. The treetops swayed and the sky looked ominous. It would be best to head out for some exercise straight after breakfast if they were to beat the rain. Shelby dressed Caity in warm clothes and rubber boots, and they set off toward the back boundary, the dogs racing ahead.

In the distance, someone was at work on the honey farm. Impulsively telling the dogs to stay back, Shelby secured the gate and crossed the flat paddocks toward a figure draped in netting and bulky clothes. Caity took one look at the alarming hood and screamed, just as Lexi pulled off her protective head gear, offering a friendly smile to Caity and exchanging names with her before accounting for her attire.

'These are beehives,' she explained. 'I have to be careful I don't upset the bees or they might fly out and sting me.'

'Were you going to collect honey?' Shelby asked.

'No. We don't take it during the winter. Without blossoms, bees live on what they've stored. I'm just checking the hives. Last year we lost two with beetle infestation.'

They strolled toward the house.

'How is Blade settling in?'

'He's fine. I plan to move him from the stable today, and put him in with Fernando.'

She indicated an old grey pony in a separate paddock, and smiled at the little girl in the oversized hat. 'Would you like a pony ride?'

Caity nodded shyly.

'Don't worry!' Lexi sensed Shelby was hesitant. 'Fernando will only walk. He's not going to bolt. Let's pick up a halter. Ông Ngoai will be happy to meet your daughter.'

It felt too complicated to Shelby to explain that she was minding Nathan's child. As they came up to the veranda, the old man was sitting as though he hadn't moved since her last visit. He waved, and drew Caity's attention to the basket beside his chair. She shook her head and backed away, until he bent and scooped up a newborn kitten, holding it out in his wrinkled palm.

'They were only born last night,' said Lexi.

Caity was unable to resist, and reached out to touch the blind scrap of fur, her dainty fingers a poignant contrast to the weathered old hand holding the kitten. As he returned it to its watchful mother, Lexi rearranged his blanket.

'Ông Ngoai has always been kind and

patient with children and animals. It's why I like to look after him now.'

Pointing to the scudding clouds, the old man spoke in Vietnamese.

'He's saying there's a weather change on the way. He thinks I need to cover the hives.'

Speaking to him in their language, she went into the house, returning with a halter.

'Let's see to that pony ride first.'

Looking at the little girl sitting importantly astride Fernando, Shelby felt a throb of happiness. And, as she watched her small charge race home through the lush grass after her ride, her face flushed with accomplishment, she couldn't have felt more pride if Caity really had been her own child. Perhaps, with her help, Caity could find her way back to a normal life again.

* * *

As Nathan swung into the driveway and pulled up, Shelby saw the little girl race to the vehicle, her steps exuberant. Her father stepped out to ruffle her hair and listen to her news. But something must be wrong. His body stiffened. He said something sharply. Caity was stepping back, an expression of dismay on her face as she watched him stride toward the steps. As he stood in the kitchen doorway, his anger physical in its intensity, Shelby had a flash of that stranger she'd first seen on the beach. Then, his size, his darkness, his remote aura had taken the form of her savior. Now he was her accuser. She stepped back in alarm. What had she done?

'You allowed Caity to ride a horse? You realize she could have fallen off and killed herself?'

'Nathan! We wandered over to the honey farm to see Lexi. All she did was offer for Caity to sit on the old horse. She kept hold of the halter. It was only a short walk in the paddock!'

'Without a child's helmet? If I'd had any idea you'd take such a crazy risk, I would never have placed her in your care.'

His eyes had the greenish glint of ice as he swung back to Caity, who stood looking up at him, her expression bewildered.

'Unless I'm with you, don't ever get on a horse again. Do you understand?'

'Nathan! You're frightening her! She was perfectly safe.'

He took another step toward Shelby, closing the space between them.

She saw the adamant set of his mouth. She didn't deserve such a scene. He didn't respect her, that much was obvious. As far as he was concerned, she was a temporary nursemaid, and the quicker he found a professional, the happier he'd be. She would be superfluous, and the little girl whose trust she was slowly earning, day by day, would transfer her affection to someone with proper credentials.

Nathan's cutting judgment of her was unfair and hurtful. Really hurtful. She'd tried so hard, and he was telling her she'd failed. What worried her more was the effect he was having on his daughter. Shelby knew plenty about over-protective parents — enough to warn Nathan his reaction was over the top.

'Nathan, you can't protect her from everything!'

'I can try.'

'You won't allow her to go swimming with her classmates, in case she drowns? You won't let her have a bicycle, in case she has an accident? You'll stop her having boyfriends because they might treat her badly and break her heart? Nathan, life's not safe! Not for anybody. The only way to be safe is to lock yourself away, keep your heart on ice, never feel. Maybe then you'll be safe. But you won't be living, either.'

Without a word, he swung on his heel and walked away, his footsteps ringing on the wooden floorboards. Shelby heard his door slam. How dare he accuse her of neglecting Caity! She'd been extremely careful. The old sway-backed horse had taken a few slow steps, that was all. Just enough to fill Caity with a sense of accomplishment. But Nathan hadn't bothered to check the details, any more than he cared that she'd done the shopping, washed his shirts, was making his dinner. He was just one more man who took her for granted — a man she'd built up into a hero because he happened to be in the right place at the right time and he'd saved her life. Of course she was grateful. But thinking that fated meeting was the start of anything special was pure fantasy. She'd had enough of men like that. The Trevors, the Jasons, the Internet scammer, now Nathan . . . And she was going to tell him so. Right now. Shelby's pupils dilated and her deep blue irises snapped with furious sparks as she marched down the hall and pushed open his door.

The angry words welling up, burning on her lips, simply died.

Nathan was sitting on the side of the bed, his head buried in his hands in an attitude of such hopelessness she was wrenched with pity. He seemed to be on the edge of some dangerous chasm of despair. He wasn't weeping but she thought it would be better if he was. At least venting his pain might give him some relief. As it was, walled off from everything, he looked unreachable, and she did not dare approach him.

He knew she was there, but he would not look at her or speak. She stood frozen, unable either to offer comfort or withdraw. She wished that Caity or the dogs would come and interrupt. The silence was overpowering. Seconds dragged on like minutes. At last he spoke a gruff, guttural sentence, torn from his closed throat.

'Leave me alone.'

'No.'

How could she simply walk out and leave this man? Her own needs forgotten, she stood waiting for some signal, anything, to guide her. Whatever he needed was all that counted right now. Slowly, carefully, she took a step, and another, until she stood in front of his bowed torso. She waited, uncertain what to offer. Without a word, without looking up, slowly, then urgently, his arms wrapped around her and his head sank to press into her soft abdomen. Then he held her, like a comfort, like a support, and she stayed very still, knowing she would stand there as long as he needed — a minute, an hour, all night, while he absorbed her kindness and accepted comfort.

Another minute ticked by. It seemed like an hour. Inhaling a slow, shuddering breath, he drew his arms away and looked up blankly into her caring gaze.

'I thought I was over the worst of it. Since Caity arrived, it's hit me like a ton of bricks.' His tone had a note of disbelief.

'You mean Samantha?' She felt diffident. Even using his wife's name seemed intrusive.

'My wife. The mother of my child. My love. I mean . . . ' He struggled to find words.

'What I'm trying to say is, my life's

never going to be the same. Ever. How do I deal with it?'

She didn't know. But he wasn't asking her for answers. In a way he was talking to himself.

She did know that a minute ago they'd crossed a line. Nathan had allowed her to see him, really see him in the depths of his grief and pain. He'd turned to her as a woman. They'd shared true intimacy. So what if he was already standing up, pushing at his hair in some tidying gesture, as though he wanted to return to ordinary matters?

'Enough of my misery.'

Yes, he was already trying to smile, to turn the exchange into a melodrama. She knew better and had no intention of pushing him. It must have been desperately hard to reveal himself like that. Now he wanted it back to everyday ordinary. He could have whatever he needed.

'Hungry? We're having fish and chips. And Caity made red jelly.'

'Where is she, anyway? I think I

should tell her I'm sorry for flying off the deep end like that.'

'Playing with Skip and Lily. Skip ran off with her security T-shirt today. There was quite a tug-of-war. I'm afraid the shirt ripped in half. Will you call her in for dinner?'

After eating, they washed up the dishes and viewed the six o'clock news. Once Caity was in bed, Nathan showered, said goodnight and closed his bedroom door as usual. But tonight she did not have the feeling he was shutting her out. He was dealing with powerful emotions and there was nothing she could do but leave him to find his own way out of the maze.

* * *

While Nathan waited for a break in the city-bound morning traffic, he took a moment to push a worn '90's Country tape into the obsolete deck of the Patrol. He joined in, humming softly to John Williamson's easy vocals. That painful exchange in the bedroom last evening had been a wake-up call. He was taking far too much for granted. Life wasn't just about Nathan Monroe's suffering. Yes, Samantha was gone and he'd lost his wife. But Caity had lost her mother. Barbara had lost her daughter, as well as her husband. Nothing was going to change that. He hadn't really thanked Barbara for the enormous help she'd been to him and Caity. The way he was treating Shelby was unfair. It was hardly her fault if the sweet scent of her talc stirred his senses after she'd bathed, or that he felt like running a mile, rather than admit he could ever want another woman. He was lucky she hadn't walked out and left him to sort out his own problems.

He didn't know how he would manage without her. The employment agencies he'd phoned hadn't been encouraging. They were staffed by health professionals, not live-in nannies. The best they could suggest was to place an advertisement in the paper.

Quite frankly he'd be diffident about handing over his dog to a stranger, much less his precious daughter.

He intended to speak to Trevor as soon as the head vet came in to work. If it was true that a merger was in the offing, then Nathan had been hired under a false assumption and that changed everything. He wasn't a pawn on someone's business chessboard and he certainly wasn't going to hang around while his locum's role was evaluated. Shelby's low opinion of her boss might be justified.

Purposefully he revved the vehicle and eased into a break in the lane. Sitting around brooding was not his nature. It was time to get off his butt and act, before that precious young woman slipped through his fingers. As soon as he arrived at work, he confronted Trevor, who saw nothing unethical in his secretive plans.

'I don't see the problem.' Trevor was matter-of-fact. 'The Bayside practice would bring their own client list with them and our catchment area would double. We could only benefit. They have state-of-the-art diagnostic equipment and their ambulance is brand new.'

'And my appointment?'

'You were only hired for six months,' Trevor reminded him.

The evasive choice of words rankled.

'I want a straight answer, Trevor. Will I still have a job?'

'I can't see why you wouldn't be employed. You've worked with large animals. There are farms and racing stables on Bayside's books.'

'So none of the present staff would be compromised? What about Shelby?'

'It would depend on who they bring from their existing practice.'

This was going nowhere. They were interrupted by the new receptionist, who had stepped smoothly into her duties, and showed no sign of relinquishing Shelby's puppy training class. Now she tapped on Trevor's door, explaining a woman had reported a distressed kangaroo stranded in her back yard, which opened onto a main highway fringed by a bush reserve.

'Tell her to ring the RSPCA or Wildlife Rescue. It's really none of our business . . . '

Nathan interrupted Trevor's dismissing words. 'Is the woman still on the line? I'll speak to her.'

He quickly established that the location was near the clinic, programed the address into his GPS and drove away. He was familiar with this scenario. New subdivisions built on the existing pathways of native animals could cause real problems for wildlife. Someone was urgently needed to steer the animal away from the dangerous road and back into the bush it had evidently wandered from. The clients waiting for him to clip nails and administer worm tablets could wait. An animal's life was at stake here.

He sped through streets of recently-built homes and pulled up at the end of a cul-de-sac. The worried caller was waiting as he parked. She beckoned and he followed her to the back garden, where the kangaroo was barely visible beneath the leafy camouflage of bushes near her back boundary. A panicked dash by the powerful animal into the traffic would not only endanger its life but probably cause an accident or vehicle pile-up. Avoiding its lethal kicking legs and claws, Nathan took his time, moving cautiously. He positioned himself to grab its tail close to its rump, while using his own body to block the kangaroo's escape toward the busy road. He steered the animal in the direction of the reserve before it took off, bounding back toward its hidden grazing grounds.

'I'd get that section of the yard fenced off,' Nathan advised the grateful woman. 'This is a fairly new subdivision. Bush kangaroos probably used this ground as a natural corridor. They'll keep coming back, until their joeys grow up and learn to follow new paths.'

'Is there a fee?'

He shook his head. This wasn't a veterinary call. Strictly speaking. Trevor was within his rights to refuse assistance. Other agencies existed to assist native animals, but in this case Nathan had enough experience to understand that speed had been essential. Disoriented and out of its normal habitat, a kangaroo was prone to stress myopathy, which would lead to organ shutdown and death. Trevor surely knew that. Apparently he didn't care.

Nathan's sense of achievement dwindled as he arrived back at the clinic, where he guessed Trevor would have something to say. He slammed the door of the Patrol and strode across the car park, simmering anger coming to the boil as the practice nurse told him the head vet wanted to see him immediately. He wasn't a naughty kid, about to be handed a detention. He rarely allowed his temper to vent, but the pressures of recent days were becoming too much. He couldn't get the memory of last night's events out of his head. He'd shouted at Shelby — virtually accused her of incompetence. Like some sooky child he'd cried, actually grabbed her and cried his eyes out. Nothing had been said. She hadn't asked for an apology and he hadn't offered one. But what must she think of him?

Well, one thing was sure. He wasn't going to fall apart for Trevor! He didn't regret his action one bit. If a few clients had to sit and wait, too bad. Ignoring his summons, he went straight to a consulting room and called the next patient.

* * *

For once, Shelby was glad her time with Nathan and his daughter was nearly over. She'd let herself drift into some insidious dream of a world where she was indispensable. True, Nathan needed a replacement wife and Caity needed a mother. Last night had made Shelby's own role plain. Second best. She was a handy substitute while a grieving man and his unsettled daughter sorted out their future. Which left her exactly nowhere.

Or was she rationalizing, believing she was simply lending a hand, helping out? There was a reason she'd been so willing to step in and help. Yes, she'd had a large bill to pay and Nathan's offer had been convenient. But a mysterious connection had been formed, weeks earlier, when he'd appeared and saved her life. She'd had the strangest conviction then that they were meant to be together. It was almost as though she knew his features and his ways from some other time.

She'd stood there last night, her arms holding him, his clasping her like a lifeline. There'd been no motive of desire, no sexual pull. No, something that ran even deeper had bound them close and everything else could wait. At the very edge of despair he'd clung to her and she'd pulled him through the darkness, back into the world.

She had to stop thinking about Nathan. He wasn't going to beg her to stay. What could she say, even if he did? Everything else in her life would have to go — her job, her dreams of travel. Other people seemed so certain about their course. If they took a training course, they passed the exams and obtained the certificate. If they planned a trip, they made bookings and they went. It was time Shelby decided what she wanted, and stopped waiting for romance.

Pulling out of her introspective mood, she bundled Caity into warm clothing and walked over the sodden paddocks to see Lexi. Now here was a sensible woman! She did not seem to resent a life based in duty and caring. She appeared to be happy.

But as she approached the house, she could hear the shrill tones of an argument. Although she could not understand the words it was evident that Lexi was angry with her grandfather.

'Stubborn old man!' She had switched to English as she saw Shelby. 'You see the weather report? The cold wind and the rain? So what does he do? Goes wandering, no coat, no shoes, his slippers all wet from the long grass. What is he doing? Trying to lift the bee hives and carry them to high ground. What did the doctor tell him? No heavy lifting, no strain. What am I to do with him?'

Throughout this tirade, the old man assumed an attitude of polite incomprehension. Still muttering, Lexi brought out a change of clothing and dry shoes and socks. Stripping her grandfather like a child, she tugged a woolen singlet and thick shirt over his head and did up his buttons.

'Now I bring your rice noodles, broth and vegetables. Eat! Do you want to die?'

Once he was obediently sipping the hot soup, Lexi relaxed. 'Worse than a child, I tell you!' She smiled then at Caity. 'I don't mean you, little one. Have you come for another pony ride?' She smiled down at Caity, who just looked confused and crouched down to examine the basket of kittens. Lexi turned enquiring eyes on Shelby, beckoning her into the kitchen where she set out cups and opened a packet of biscuits. Needing to talk, Shelby told her what had happened.

'Her father was being protective,' Lexi said diplomatically. 'Somehow I assumed Caity was your daughter. So you're just minding her?'

'Until Nathan hires a permanent nanny.'

'And that will be . . . '

'Soon. When my holidays end.' Even saying it out loud caused a physical pang.

'And after that you won't stay with your partner?'

'Nathan's not my partner.' Shelby shared the story of their coincidental meeting. Lexi's smile was understanding.

'But you wish he was?'

'His heart's elsewhere.'

She hadn't meant to stray into her personal life but Lexi seemed pleased to talk of something other than her grandfather's self-willed ways.

'Nathan's already married?' She sounded quite unjudging. Shelby shook her head.

'It might be easier if he was. I'd know where I stood. His wife died six months ago. Nathan's still in love with her.'

'That's perhaps a good thing? He's not a superficial man. Time will bring healing.'

'I don't have time!'

'Then enjoy what remains. Why not go out with him? Suggest a meal together, somewhere with a nice atmosphere. I will come and baby-sit for you.'

'Would you really? That's half the problem, you see. Whenever Nathan and I get together, there's always something more pressing we have to deal with. If we went out alone, perhaps we'd have the chance to really talk.' Already she was planning a night out. She'd wear something special, really go all out to impress him.

'Let's exchange phone numbers now,'

said Lexi. 'You can tell me what night you want to go. I'm always available.' Her tone was wry.

Ông Ngoai called out and she stood up.

'All day he sits and watches the clouds. He predicts much rain. He has an idea in his head that we might be flooded. It's happened before, when the river's burst its banks.'

'I'm sure Nathan could lend a hand if you need to move the hives or relocate the horses. He went through those shocking floods in Queensland. He knows all about it.'

Without going into the details of Samantha's drowning, she gave a shiver.

'I think we'll wait and see.'

Patience seemed to be her guide. Surely it must be hard, living this isolated existence with only an old man for company?

'Do you get lonely, Lexi?'

'Why think about that? When Ông Ngoai says it's time, he will return to

Vietnam to complete his cycle. Then my own life will change.'

As Shelby walked home with Caity, she decided there was merit in believing life followed its own rhythms and patterns. The drab wattle tree beside the house had suddenly burst forth into bloom, sprays of golden blossom bringing a glow to the winter landscape. As she passed the window, she picked a few stems to decorate the house. The changes she'd experienced in such a short time surely bore out that Asian idea of acceptance. True, she'd seen another side of Lexi today and wasn't sorry to understand her new friend could feel as frustrated and irritable as Shelby did at times. It made them more equal. Even so . . . All the wishing and hoping in the world was just a waste of energy. The future would unfold as it did.

7

Shelby, wearing jeans and a crimson sweater, was waiting for Nathan as he pulled up at the farmhouse. She ran down the steps as he stepped out of the vehicle.

'I was starting to worry. You're late.'

'Sorry. Not the best conditions for driving. The wind's getting up and the low-lying areas are starting to flood.'

'According to the news, this is only the fringe of the weather. I'd hate to be in the direct path!' Even as she spoke, a burst of slanting rain sent them hurrying to the house.

'I hope the house stands up okay. I'm starting to wonder why renting an old place in the middle of nowhere was a good idea.'

They went inside, where Caity was sitting near the fireplace, the torn shirt beside her and the old hat on her head.

At least she'd stopped wearing it to bed. She was brushing Lily's newly-growing coat, lecturing her on keeping it clean, while the white dog lay submissively content. Skip, abandoned in the warmth, had rolled onto his back, his paws in the air and his mouth open in a blissful grin.

Shelby filled the next half hour with domestic doings while Nathan turned on the weather channel. The wooden structure of the old house moved with the wind, sighing and creaking as gusts found loose boards and whistled through the roof cavity. Bursts of rain clattered on the iron roof, yet inside the space felt warm and safe. Aromas drifted from the kitchen as she served the evening meal.

Nathan's display of emotion the previous night had hit her like a flash of lightning. She'd seen the depth of his conflict and understood he was in no state to look for a new relationship. Lexi's way of accepting things seemed the only course. In a week, she was supposed to resume her work at the clinic. Nathan's decisions after that would be none of her concern.

Still, Caity's future had to be discussed. She waited until they'd eaten and the dishes were stacked in the sink.

'Nathan. We need to talk.'

He nodded. 'I'll get Caity tucked up.'

He walked down the hall, carrying his daughter. Distantly she could hear laughter and soon the words of some bedtime story. Shelby went back to sit by the fire, a knot building in her solar plexus as the minutes ticked by. His display of grief had only deepened her connection to him.

His footsteps sounded, loud on the wooden floor.

'Would you like a glass of wine?'

Wine! She'd stored a couple of bottles in the back of a kitchen cupboard, but he'd never suggested they should share one.

'I guess so.'

'Red or white?'

'White, please.'

Her fingertips tingled as he handed her the glass. The ruddy flames burnished his brown hair as he sat down beside her.

She took a gulp of wine. 'Would you like to go out to dinner one night? Lexi offered to come and babysit for us.'

She half-expected him to knock back the invitation. He just nodded. 'Nice of her. Why not? If you want to.'

That was hardly a clear message. She had to clarify things and repeated herself. 'Nathan, we need to talk.'

'We do.' She saw he was smiling, his expression rueful. 'I wish I was better at it. I haven't been honest with you.' He sounded reflective. 'Actually I haven't been honest with myself.'

'What do you mean?' The questions in Shelby's mind spilled out. 'I'm confused, Nathan. We met under such strange circumstances. I felt it was fate, especially when you showed up again at the clinic. Now I'm living with you! It's temporary, I know. But tell me one thing. What do you want?'

He was sitting close enough that she could see the specks of green and gold in his hazel eyes.

'What do I want?' He sounded surprised. Why was he so slow to make his feelings known? Surely he could see she longed to be more than a housekeeper and minder to his child? Emotion darkened her eyes and her voice broke.

'Yes! What do you want from me? You act aloof, then sometimes you're so . . . It's as though you care.'

Nathan placed a finger under her chin, traced the curve of her flushed cheek. With the pad of his thumb he gently wiped away a tear. But her heart sank at his next words.

'I've been carrying this false picture about my marriage. Samantha . . . '

'Don't talk about Samantha!' Now she was angry, hearing yet again the name of a ghost she could never hope to compete with. 'I'm sorry for your pain, Nathan, but I can't help the fact your wife is dead.' She leaned away from him, unable to bear his fixation on a past she didn't share with him. 'I can't help you. I hope you can get over her in time. I have my own life to live. We ought to discuss Caity's care when I go back to work next week.'

'Shelby, I need to tell you this! The day Sam went, we had a big fight. I couldn't drop my work and go, whenever she snapped her fingers. Sam always made the rules. And I followed. Even leaving New Zealand wasn't my choice . . . '

'Nathan, I don't care! So you were in love. It was your choice. Don't you think I've made impulsive decisions and then blamed other people for my own mistakes? I'm tired of hearing about your wife; what a wonderful daughter, what a great mother, such a marvelous wife you will never be able to love again!'

He was looking at her intently, his expression inscrutable. Was he upset? Her dismissive outburst had shocked her. Yet she felt a swell of relief, as though she'd escaped from a tricky pathway where every step must be negotiated with care. Her anger had made them equals. Unless Nathan stopped treating her as a handy fallback, she meant exactly what she'd said. She had her own life to lead, with or without him, and suddenly she knew she would be perfectly fine.

'Will you let me say one thing, Shelby?' She nodded and he took her hand. 'I don't want you to go. Please stay. We need you. Both of us. Will you stay?'

His sincerity was genuine, and shock raced through her blood, warning her she was at a major crossroads. How had Nathan and Caity taken over her life so suddenly? She'd only met them a few short weeks ago. Sensibly, she should sit down and examine the consequences of his offer. Her answer would affect everything from her career to her dreams of travel. Perhaps her entire life.

Nathan hesitated. 'I'm not trying to influence you but there's one thing I should mention. I'm not sure how secure our jobs will be. There's some kind of merger underway. Trevor confirmed that to me today.'

She was silent. In a way she wasn't surprised to hear the news. Trevor always had his own agenda. But if she became Caity's nanny, it would be through choice, not because she needed a job.

'That wouldn't influence me, Nathan.'

He was waiting. Was she reading it right? Did he really want to? He moved closer. Gently his lips found hers, promising her they could afford all the good will and time in the world to erase his memories and resolve her choices.

* * *

A tremendous bang overhead quenched the feelings their kiss had aroused. Torn back from the moment when everything was about to change, they sprang to their feet.

'Check Caity!' Nathan was already

feeling for his keys and grabbing his parka from the hook in the hall. As soon as he opened the door, he was almost knocked off his feet as a violent gust of wind surged at him. The banging came again. The flashlight he kept in the vehicle showed one end of a sheet of roofing iron had been torn free. In the dim visibility it waved ominously, flapping up and down like a torn sail. It sounded as though it could sheer away at any moment. If so, rain would pour straight into the house, where the weight of water would very likely cause the old ceiling to collapse.

He ought to secure that sheet. He knew there wasn't a ladder anywhere. Starting up the Patrol, he revved hard, pulling the vehicle around to park it parallel and as close as he could get to the house. Shelby was a pale silhouette at the window.

'Stay inside!' he yelled. 'Keep Caity in my room. I'm going up to inspect the damage.'

The spotlights he'd never used for

hunting threw a hard glare on the house. If he climbed on top of the four wheel drive, he should be tall enough to get ropes onto the loose sheet and tie it down. The scene around him was like a disaster movie, with hissing bursts of rain, swaying trees, and the howl of the gusts that fringed a full-blown cyclone to the north.

Shelby was calling again from the window. 'The power's just gone off. There could be lines down. Be careful, Nathan!'

Be careful? He grinned, even as he knew the dangers that were inevitable in weather like this. How could you be careful when you were slipping and sliding on a wet roof rack, the wind throwing punches like a boxer, and a sheet of lethal iron threatening to decapitate you at any moment? He lurched back as the iron banged again, bringing a splintered roof strut with it. His mind worked methodically, thinking of options. If he could just get a tie-down on that strut and hitch it to the roof rack . . . Working as well as he could in the poor light, he climbed back down to firm ground, collected his ropes, and spent the next ten minutes clambering up and down in a fruitless attempt to stabilize the iron. There was nothing to fix the rope to, and he lacked tools and light to see what he was doing. Reluctantly he shelved that idea. All he could do was make sure nobody was at risk if the ceiling did give way. The rest would have to wait till morning.

Wet, muddy and heated by the adrenaline rush, Nathan was energized. Action swept away all those sad, worrying memories, and pulled him into the present where his priority now was keeping his family dry and safe until the damage could be assessed in the morning.

Firelight still cast a glow over the living room. A gentle illumination glimmered from Shelby's bedroom, where she was waiting for him, his daughter curled up in a drowsy heap with the dogs.

'There's nothing I can do tonight,' Nathan said. 'Sorry, it's going to be a disturbed night, with that banging. But at least we're dry.' He noticed a delicate perfume as he stood in the doorway, looking around. 'Where did you find the candles?'

'I had a couple in my packing.' She did not say she'd bought them when she'd once had ideas of a romantic evening with Justin. They'd remained stored away, never lit until tonight.

'You're a good Girl Guide. Well prepared!'

He must look like a derelict with his hair soaked and his clothes dripping water all over the floor. Yet Shelby was gazing up at him, her lips parted, her glowing eyes reflecting an emotion he could only call adoring.

'Nathan, you look just the way you were on the beach, the day you saved me.'

In spite of himself he felt flattered. No woman had ever looked at him with such devotion, as though he really was a hero in her eyes. What might have happened, out there by the fire, if that sheet of iron hadn't interrupted them? Wet and dripping as he was, his body stirred at the memory of her yielding lips and her soft body melting in his arms. Was he really ready to move into a new relationship? He could see Samantha's cold image in her coffin and a shiver ran through him. He should be grateful for the storm. The last thing he intended was to mislead Shelby. She didn't need a man whose memory was scarred with confusion and pain. She might think he was a hero, but he knew better.

'I'll get dry and go to bed. The bedrooms are safe enough. The kitchen might be affected, if that iron reefs right off during the night.'

'Caity won't want to sleep alone,' she pointed out.

'She can share with me.'

He had to stamp out his urge to be drawn by the lure of the candlelight. Her gaze spoke to him, inviting him to step into the room and resume where they'd left off. Turning abruptly, he walked away.

* * *

Shelby sank back against the pillows, cradling the sleeping child against her. The candles threw flickering shadows on the wall. The wind rattled the window frame and the tree branch tapped and scraped against the glass. Overhead, the loose iron delivered shuddering bangs. As Nathan had said, they were certainly in for a disturbed night. He was the most contradictory man! One minute romantic, the next rejecting. If this was his usual way of showing a woman he cared, she wasn't surprised that his wife had been packing her cases for a long visit elsewhere! Seeing him standing in the half-light, that same dark-clothed apparition who still came to her in her dreams, she knew he was her ideal man. Of course he was good-looking. Yes, he was intelligent, strong, and decisive, but her heart called out to something so much deeper than those outer things. When Nathan saved her life, he'd laid claim to her, and she had given herself to him, body and soul. The thought of life without him was unbearable.

The yellow flashlight bobbed past her door. She could hear him moving around in his bedroom, probably changing into dry clothes. The partition between their rooms had never seemed so flimsy. Outside, the storm increased in ferocity, with jagged snaps of lightning throwing weird shadows that sent Skip into frenzies of barking. Lily, who was partly deaf, snored on while Caity snuggled closer.

The light shone at her door, framing his dark silhouette.

'Shall I take Caity now?'

'I don't mind if she stays with me. I'm not going to get any sleep.'

'Are you worried? We're safe enough.'

She wished he'd stay. How could she say she felt like a child, wanting company, needing someone strong to stay with her and keep away the dark?

'I'm fine,' she lied.

'I'll say goodnight, then. See you in the morning.'

She wished she had that kind of sang froid, to hop into bed, close her eyes and drift off to sleep, never mind the turmoil outside. She wriggled lower under the covers, comforting herself with Caity's warmth and the snuffles of Lily. Skip secretively levered himself aboard to join them, circling to curl up at her feet. In a kind of trance, half-awake, half-asleep, she let herself float into romantic fantasy, remembering the want Nathan had stirred up in her with his embrace and kiss. What was he thinking about now, stretched out alone in his bed? The erotic moments they'd shared, and where they might lead?

The intermittent thunder was softer, a low grumble moving away, though the rain showed no sign yet of easing. She thought there were longer intervals between the wind gusts that suddenly blew up, whistling through the old building's crevices. Almost on the verge of sleep, she relaxed and her breathing found the natural rhythm of rest.

A horrible thump and the shattering of glass jerked her wide awake in a second. Freezing rain blew through the broken windowpane, where the uprooted wattle tree must have landed.

This was like a home invasion; sudden, unexpected and terrifying. For a moment she wondered if the whole wall was about to collapse, burying her along with Caity.

Lily and Skip had prudently bolted. Shelby leapt out of bed, grabbed Caity, and bumped into Nathan at the door.

'Are you okay? What the hell happened?' Swiftly he assessed the damage. 'You'll have to sleep in my room. We can't do much about this till the morning.' He was shifting her furniture out of the rain as he spoke. 'I can sleep on the couch.'

'Please Nathan!' She felt on the verge

of nervous tears. 'This is silly! Can't we be together? You don't need to sleep on the couch. I'm not going to attack you!'

'Shelby!' Was he laughing? His voice sounded that way. 'Believe me, I'm far more inclined to attack you! I'm having a terrible struggle to keep my hands off you. You must know that.'

Taking Caity from her arms, he carried the child into his room and settled her in the bed. Then he turned, gathering Shelby to him and laying her down beside his sleeping daughter.

'Do you know what a beautiful woman you are? Looks like we're fated to go to bed together.'

He spoke lightly enough, but she knew he had reservations.

'Don't worry! We have a built-in chaperone,' she said, matching his mood as he brought the candles from her bedroom and climbed in beside her. He was only wearing boxers and a T-shirt. The feel of his body was so exactly right. With Caity beside them, of course nothing could happen tonight. Yet his strong male presence, his smell, the silk of his skin and the brush of the curling hair on his forearms filled her with longing. How easily she could turn to him, inviting him to explore her body, tempting him to forget control and simply take her. Her lips were so close to him, her arms encircled him, his body pressed against her with quickening desire.

'This is so nice,' she whispered, as his hand smoothed the soft contour of her waist and hips.

'Too nice,' he murmured, turning her over so he could stroke his fingers up and down her back. 'Much too nice.'

As he pulled her bottom against his hips with a groan of frustration, she sighed with pleasure.

Something like a miracle was happening to her. Eager desire was replacing the distaste a man's touch usually stirred in her. She drowsed and woke, feeling Nathan's hands fondle and caress her. The long erotic night seemed endless. Finally, near dawn, she drifted into a deeper sleep, only waking when shafts of sunlight fell across her pillow. She reached for Nathan and Caity but the bed was empty. For a time she lay in a daydream, reliving the eventful night. The pit of her stomach felt heavy and engorged from the arousal that had built. Of course there had been no release, with Caity beside them, tossing and restless. Just darkness, and the slow, arousing friction of limbs and bodies, man and woman, desire and want.

Where was the little girl now? Perhaps Nathan had taken her with him while he assessed the damage. Fastening the buttons of her pajama top, she went to the window. The only noises now were invisible birds and the aggressive crowing of a rooster right outside the window. Lexi's chicken coop must have collapsed. Her small flock would be roaming free.

Shelby stretched with feline laziness. Tiptoeing to avoid broken glass, she checked her own room. In daylight, she could see the wattle tree had smashed into the window, its shallow root system upended like a bizarre Afro. Grabbing the first clean clothes she could reach, she was dressing when her mobile phone rang. She could see it, lying near a pool of rainwater on top of her dressing table. Surprised it was still working, she answered and heard Lexi's voice.

'Are you looking for your white dog? She's sitting on my veranda, very wet and bedraggled. And my rooster's gone.'

'He's here, king of the castle.'

'Don't pick him up. He's a mean bird! I'll come and get him, and bring your dog home.'

'I'll put the kettle on. I need a coffee.'

'The electricity's still down,' Lexi reminded her.

Shelby groaned. 'Maybe I can light the fire. I'll come down and meet you at the back fence.' She dragged on a sweater and jeans and went outside. Peace had replaced the din of last night's storm. The clear sky and pleasant breeze were a mute backdrop to the whipped trees hung with tattered bark, and the broken branches sprawled around the yard. The wattle tree slumped against the house. Near the back gate, one large tree had flattened a section of fencing, leaving the gap that Lily had no doubt discovered.

There was still no sign of Nathan, Caity or Skip. Concerned, Shelby called their names but there was no reply.

* * *

Hugging his soaked daughter, Nathan stood staring at the swollen creek. Water spilled over Lexi's property, forming shallow lakes on the low-lying ground. The horses must have been moved into the stables, higher up. A lone white hen pecked busily around the puddles.

Caity was crying. She'd been standing thigh-deep in the creek when Nathan saw her. His frantic reaction had been to swoop on her and scoop her up as though truck wheels were about to crush her. He'd frightened her, and made things worse by scolding her for running away. Now he felt pain in the back of his throat, as though guilt was trying to escape. He'd turned his back for what, a minute? Just to collect a few tools to try and secure the fence. Wait there, sweetheart. I'll only be a moment . . . And Caity had disappeared, apparently chasing Lily, who must have discovered the gap and taken off. Skip had stayed, barking, and as soon as Nathan appeared, had headed toward the creek.

Nathan wished now he could undo his crazy dash and his shouts. Caity's pajamas were soaked and her muffled sobs cut him with regret.

Pulling her close, he slowed his pace. 'I'm not cross,' he said. 'I was just so afraid when you were gone. What were you doing at the creek? It's not a safe place for you.'

'I chased Lily. She ran away. My hat blew in the creek. It's gone.' Her tears began again in earnest.

'Your hat!' He hugged her thankfully. 'We'll buy you a new hat, Caity.'

'No-o-o-o!'

Her sobs grew louder until she was distracted by the sight of an energetic, waving woman coming toward them, Lily at her heels.

'Lexi! She found Lily!'

Caity wriggled to be set down. She set off at a run, stumbling over the sodden paddock, while Nathan watched, his chest tight with anxiety. That moment when he'd seen his precious daughter wading out into the creek had terrified him. Had some quirk of fate chosen him to be a victim of accidents around water? His wife, his father-in-law, Shelby's near-drowning in the sea, now Caity — and here he was, daring to think he was a good bet for a relationship with Shelby. Last night had stunned him. He'd never known such desire, not just to satisfy himself, but to give to this caring woman who so patiently put up with his contradictory emotions. He'd looked at her sleeping, her breathing soft and regular, and actually thought he was ready to love again. But his momentary lapse in attention could well have led to another loss, another tragedy. How could he ask Shelby to ride such a dangerous roller coaster? Best he steer clear of relationships. He was a Jonah, and surely enough damage had been done.

Shelby was waiting by the damaged fence as he strode toward her, Lexi following.

'We haven't met,' the Asian woman acknowledged, 'but Shelby's often mentioned you. I see you've had some damage too.'

He welcomed the small talk. The personal way Shelby was touching his arm made him think of the long night they'd shared, and he mustn't go there. He'd misled her quite enough last night.

'We had a sheet blow off the roof, and this mess needs fixing.' He indicated the fallen tree and broken fence. 'Did you have any major damage?'

'The chicken coop's a heap of rubble and we have trees down, too.'

She seemed a pleasant woman, and

Shelby had told him about the dutiful care she gave her grandfather. Running that big property alone must be hard.

'I'll give you a hand later, if you like. Have you got a chain saw?'

As Lexi smiled at him, he saw Shelby glance from him to his daughter, her expression mystified.

'Why is Caity drenched?'

'She had a slight accident. She's fine.'

How could he say he'd let a four-year-old wander into a flooded creek? He indicated the fallen tree and scattered branches. 'I'm going to start cleaning up and do something about the roof.'

'Surely you'll have something to eat first?' Shelby was touching him again, no doubt waiting for some response after the sweet night they'd shared. He had to stick to his decision.

'Not hungry, thanks.' The look on her face was killing him. He turned and strode up the yard, started the Patrol and headed to the hardware store.

* * *

'A man of action, isn't he?' Lexi spoke lightly but it was obvious Shelby was bewildered by his sudden departure. Followed by Caity and the dogs, the women picked their way through debris toward the house, where Shelby chained Lily and Skip, and Lexi located her rooster.

'I can't stay,' she said. 'Ông Ngoai will be wanting his breakfast. After he's eaten, you're welcome to use my little primus stove. I'll bring it over.'

Thanking her, Shelby pulled off Caity's drenched pajamas and dried her, trying to ignore her full-blown tantrum. She refused to have her hair brushed or her shoelaces tied, and threw her plate of Weetabix on the floor. It took a full hour to settle her and uncover the problem of her lost hat. The psychology behind her behavior might be understandable, but coping with her left Shelby drained.

She heard the vehicle pull up beside

the house, and still Nathan did not come in to talk to her. She saw he was unloading his purchases, and within minutes the abrasive whine of a drill started up overhead. The noise, plus the dogs' mournful whines and Caity's grizzles, only added to the state of her overstretched nerves. Something serious had happened but that was no reason for Nathan to turn his back and simply walk away.

He was perched on the roof ridge, trying to secure a blue plastic tarpaulin. Even from a distance she could tell he was remote. An angry heat surged through her as she summoned him.

'Nathan! I want to talk to you!'

He went on inspecting the drill as she shouted up to him.

'Are you coming down or do I have to come up?'

He did not answer.

The heat boiled over. Furious, she hoisted herself onto the Patrol roof and looked for a way to scramble up the damaged roof.

'Don't do that! It's not safe.'

He sounded genuinely alarmed but she had a tenuous foothold and showed no sign of backing off.

'Are you going to tell me what's wrong, or should I just pack up and leave?'

'What are you talking about? Leave? Why?' He was sliding down, eye level with her.

'I don't know what last night meant to you!' she snapped. 'Apparently very little.'

'That's not right.'

'Then you've got a big problem, Nathan. Because the messages you keep sending me tell me you just don't care at all.'

His expression was thoroughly confused. 'Shelby. I do care. That's the problem. Let's get off the roof and we can talk.'

She scowled at the drill as though it symbolized all the distractions that kept them apart. 'We can talk quite well up here. You can just go back to your drilling and I can go and pack.'

'The battery's dead. I can't recharge it.'

He smiled, inviting her to defuse the argument, but she glared at him.

'I feel like pushing you off this roof, Nathan! How can you joke? I'm serious.'

'So am I. If only you knew how serious I am! I'm crazy about you.'

'You have a funny way of showing it. You just turned your back on me this morning.'

Now she was on the verge of crying, as all the stress and build-up of the storm, the night, and their relationship threatened to escape.

'We should get down before you do push me! We'll talk, I promise.'

He scrambled past her while she looked out over the yard and paddocks beyond. Up here, the viewpoint was different. Suddenly she felt detached from everyday things, as though she was on a mystery flight, travelling to an unknown destination. Where she was going or how it would end she had no idea. She'd come aboard, and now there was no stopping, no getting off midway. She could only wait and see where this journey with Nathan would end.

He was on the ground, waiting to help her down. Accepting his hand, she jumped and he hugged her.

'Is this so hard for you?' she murmured against his chest. 'Do you really want to run away?'

'I don't. Of course I don't. But I'm no good for you.'

'I'll decide that.' Her voice was muffled as he pulled her closer.

'Look at how we met, on the brink of disaster. Today I took my eyes off Caity for a minute, and the next thing she's in the creek.'

She'd guessed as much and understood why he'd reacted as he did. She thought of all the distraught owners who'd come rushing to the clinic, blaming themselves because their pet had ingested poison, picked up a tick or been stricken by some illness. Not everything could be prevented or controlled. Random accidents lurked in unexpected places. Her own near-drowning was just one example. Nathan had to believe that and she wanted to help him.

'We can deal with anything, as long as you don't shut me out.' She leaned into his arms and felt them tighten around her.

'We've got a lot of talking to do,' he agreed.

'Yes.' She surveyed the strewn yard. 'I think that can wait till tonight, don't you? Let's eat and then I'll give you a hand cleaning up.'

She savored their closeness, but wondered if they could ever resolve their conflicts.

8

So much had happened in just a few days. The storm seemed a long-ago event, and the promised talk was replaced by the mundane problems of cooking, showering and keeping warm in a household bereft of electricity. By the time power was finally restored, Nathan was caught up in emergency repairs both to his own property and to Lexi's, who'd had more damage than she first assumed. Apart from momentary eye contact or the brush of hands, Nathan and Shelby's communication revolved around practical affairs.

Shelby had her own distractions. Her parents' offer of an overseas trip, normally such an exciting prospect, had come at the worst time. Every aspect of her life was adrift, and then there was Caity. Day by day the little girl was changing. She did not mention the lost hat. Perhaps it was a blessing the water had taken her reminder of the past. She still had tantrums or bouts of sobbing, but she seemed to trust Shelby and responded to Lily, dressing her in improvised costumes and tying a ribbon in her sparse coat. How could Shelby simply vanish overseas? A child had no concept of time or space. Everything happened here and now, and if Shelby left, perhaps all the good work would be undone.

To complicate matters, Shelby's mother phoned. Her calls usually started with inquiries about her daughter's health. Her concern was genuine, but annoying, reminding Shelby of her teenage years. She'd moved on and did not need her mother's constant fussing. However, today Shirley sounded different.

'Are you okay, Mum?'

'Not really. Daddy's had bad news.'

Shelby felt her heart clutch apprehensively. 'What do you mean? Is he sick?'

'He had his regular skin check and the doctor did a biopsy of a small mole. Not much more than a freckle. The results came back yesterday. Oh Shelby, it's a melanoma.'

'Oh no! How serious is it?'

'Andrew's making light of it. The doctor's removing it as we speak. I guess it depends on what he finds.'

Shelby was aware that animals came in to the clinic with melanomas, which vets treated immediately with extensive surgery. 'When will he know the results?'

'I'm not sure. I've been doing an Internet search. I'm very worried, darling.'

'Of course. I suppose you'll cancel your trip now?'

'Andrew's adamant we should go. As far as he's concerned, this is no more than a minor interruption. He's never had a day's illness. He doesn't understand this could be life-threatening.'

'Mum, I know it's scary, but let's not go for the worst scenario.' This was a reversal of roles. She'd never had to reassure her mother before. 'Daddy may be right. Lots of people are diagnosed with melanoma and survive if it's removed in time.'

'It's good to talk to you. I feel I have to put on an act with Andrew. He can't stand me fussing. Says I'm a drama queen.'

'You do have a vivid imagination, Mum!'

'In fantasy, yes. But writing about death in a murder mystery isn't the same as facing a terminal illness in my husband.'

'Aren't you jumping the gun a bit, Mum? Let's find out how serious the situation is.'

'That's true. I'll try. Shelby, let me say one thing. We both love you very much and if we do go on this holiday, we really need you to come. Andrew will be hurt if you turn down his offer, and I need your support.' Shirley's voice broke and Shelby wished she could reach out and hug her. But she couldn't possibly make a commitment right now, as her responsibilities to the clinic, Nathan, and Caity loomed.

'When would I need to decide? It's just that I have so much going on.'

'So you said before. But surely this

puts a different light on things?'

'Yes. It does. Promise you'll let me know everything. Good news or bad. And by the time you know about the trip, I should be able to juggle things.'

'Think about it! We've never had a family trip since you . . . '

'Since I cracked up,' Shelby finished. 'I know, Mum. But that's in the past.'

Afterwards, she sat on the steps in the weak sunshine, mulling over her options. She was due back at work and rushing Caity into a day care situation felt wrong. She needed to sit down with Nathan and discuss everything, but today he'd made an early start on work at Lexi's, where the storm had inflicted damage to the stable roof as well as the chicken coop. Nathan seemed to get along well with the Asian woman. He'd made a few complimentary remarks about her kind manner toward her grandfather, and Lexi had confided in him that when the old man eventually returned to Vietnam, she hoped to set up a riding school.

Nathan was coming home for lunch, so Shelby set Caity on a chair at the counter to help mix a batch of pancakes. Perhaps while they were eating she could bring him up to date with her parents' news. As she responded to the little girl's chatter and watched the dogs scrapping over an old bone in the yard, she realized she was dreading going back to work at the clinic. Just then her cell phone rang, as though the head vet had read her mind.

Trevor launched into the news that Pelican Waters Vet Clinic was proceeding with a merger. A staff shuffle was underway.

'Of course we value your work here,' Trevor said, his tone oozing insincerity. Shelby hadn't paid much attention to Nathan's mention of a merger but now her heart began to race. He was going to sack her.

'We've decided to transfer their receptionist here. She has extra qualifications we can utilize. But we'd like you to consider taking on work at the other clinic to keep things running during the transition. We'll have a rostered skeleton staff there, to keep the local clients happy.'

That sounded interesting. She might have a job with more scope, well away from Trevor's irritating ways.

'Where is the other clinic?' It would be ideal if she and Nathan could travel in to work together. Surely before long they could arrange suitable day care for Caity?

'Weakley Flats.'

She was dumbstruck. The only Weakley Flats she knew of was at least a two hour drive from the city. Apart from the fact of a totally unsuitable location, Trevor's offer reflected the casual opinion he had of her work.

When she said nothing, he assumed she didn't know where Weakley Flats was.

'It's north of here, on the way to Port Macquarie.'

'That's a joke, Trevor! There's no way I'm doing a four or five hour round trip every day!'

'You could always move.'

He was perfectly serious. Next he'd be telling her it would be a great opportunity to improve her driving skills. It was time to talk back.

'I'm not interested. I actually have a life. Thanks, but no thanks.'

She clicked off the connection. For the second time this morning, she realized how suddenly life could change. Her mother needed her, and she'd shown Trevor she wasn't the weak person he obviously thought she was. What the future held now was anybody's guess. Her job was gone and she might have to face a family crisis of heartbreaking depth if her father's news was serious. Yet she felt strong as she went back to cooking the pancakes. She had every reason now to clarify things with Nathan — but a flash of honesty told her that first she had to decide exactly what she wanted. True, Nathan was more a man of action, decisive and quick-thinking, his deepest feelings hard to fathom — but was she any different?

She could see Nathan heading back up the property. He stopped to examine an obstacle and, using the axe he was carrying, he paused to deliver a few sturdy blows. Several trees had shed branches but fortunately only the wattle had fallen on the house and its timber was lightweight, so no major damage had resulted. While they waited for a glazier, he'd boarded up the broken window and given Shelby his bed while he slept out in the lounge. When she'd hinted she was willing to share more love-making, he'd backed off and told her they shouldn't rush things. Confused, she'd asked why? Hadn't he liked the other night? The look he'd given her then was smoldering; so hot she understood he was on the point of crossing some line that was nothing to do with a casual affair.

His restraint was infuriating, yet only made him more desirable. He'd come to her as her rescuer. He'd fit into her life as co-worker, house-mate, and friend. But now she was continually aware that he looked, smelled and acted like a well-built, sexy man. His strong physical presence invaded her mind and she could not stop thinking about those sensuous hours they'd spent together during the storm.

She ought to respect his restraint. He wasn't out for a quick fling, that was plain. At least now she could tell him she wouldn't be going back to the clinic. Perhaps that would help him sort out his priorities?

Showing Caity how to spread margarine and jam on the pancakes, Shelby made coffee and wandered down the block to call him for lunch. Intent on his job, Nathan did not notice when she paused, admiring the grace and coordination of his muscular body as he swung the axe. No wonder he liked working with large animals and had chosen that clunky vehicle to drive. The transition to city work must be hard for him. She couldn't see him staying on with Trevor, even if he was offered a permanent post.

He looked surprised as she walked up to him.

'Time for a break.'

He dropped the axe and straightened his back, rubbing himself down with the T-shirt he'd discarded on the ground. He looked and smelled utterly masculine with the sun glinting on his skin and adding lights to his sweat-streaked brown hair.

Caity was hopping about on the steps. 'Can I bring the plate now?'

'Yes, please. Let's eat outside.'

'Nathan gave a grin.' 'I'm not fit to come inside without a shower. Sure you can put up with me?'

'Quite sure.' Sitting side by side, close enough to touch, she pushed aside her impulse to reach out and run her fingers down his half-naked body.

'You were right about the merger. Trevor rang me. He offered me a job at Weakley Flats.' Seeing Nathan had never heard of the township, she explained. 'It's about two and a half hours' drive from here.'

'Bloody ridiculous! I'll resign tomorrow!'

But already she could see a funny side to the insulting suggestion, and rested a restraining hand on his arm. He was glaring as though he wanted to pick up the axe and dismember the head vet, and part of her delighted in his protective response. She was getting to know his quick temper. He was a hot-blooded man and he could flare up suddenly, but those moods never lasted.

'I'm not that upset. If you like, now I can stay on here a bit longer.'

As she'd hoped, his face brightened at once. As long as he didn't assume it would be permanent . . . unless he could convince her he was ready to move on. Lately he seemed happier and he rarely mentioned Samantha at all. But he still fiddled with that damned wedding ring! Why was he still wearing it? As far as their own relationship went, she was left in limbo.

Caity had finished eating. She squatted by one of the overgrown tire rings that had once held plants. Carefully she selected a small flower and offered it to Shelby.

'Thank you! That's so pretty.'

'I used to help Mummy grow flowers.'

She scampered back to unearth more treasures. Her dark hair, no longer unkempt and smothered by the Akubra, gleamed in the sunlight. Nathan smiled at Shelby.

'You do know what a great job you're doing with her?' Gratitude shone in his hazel eyes. 'I'd be lost, wondering how to handle her.'

'It's going to take time, Nathan. After all, losing one's mother is about as hard as it can get.'

He nodded. 'Even when you're grown up. I often think about Mum and Dad. Mum had a heart scare a few years ago. Sometimes I feel I should live closer, in case there's another crisis.'

'Have you been back to visit?'

'Not since Caity was born. Perhaps once we're settled again . . . '

'We take parents for granted, then one day we realize they won't be around forever.'

She was about to tell him about Shirley's phone call, but there was a crash as the dogs dashed up the steps, sending cups flying. Caity lost her balance and by the time the interruption was sorted, Nathan was standing up.

'I told Lexi I'd go back this afternoon and finish the coop.'

'Must you? I was hoping to have a talk.'

'Okay. Tonight then?'

She could tell that already his thoughts had drifted back to the tasks awaiting him. It wasn't the time to insist on intimate conversation. She needed to explain her own parents' situation and discuss the overseas trip. The pressure of work had been removed. Unless she accepted the chance to spend time with them, she might have regrets one day. And if Nathan was serious about resigning from the clinic, the problems of caring for Caity and the dogs would be solved.

However embarrassing it might turn out to be, she had to know his feelings for her. For her own part, she was sure she would be happy sharing a lifetime with this lovely man. If only Jasmine was here! Shelby would take great pleasure in introducing her to a man who didn't have a devious bone in his body. Sometimes Nathan could be blunt to the point of rudeness, but she knew he was fundamentally honest and genuine.

Now he bent down to hug Caity. 'Thanks, honey. That was a great lunch.'

It was amazing how the child's food fads were almost a thing of the past. When the little girl had a hand in the cooking, she was willing to taste almost anything. Watching her now as she ran off to search for flowers, Shelby remembered reading that people sometimes made a special corner of the garden into a memorial for some loved pet. Caity had nowhere to associate with her mother. No doubt that was why she'd clung so fiercely to Samantha's hat and T-shirt.

'Caity?' she called. 'Would you like to make a special garden for your Mum? We could plant some of the flowers she liked to grow, and you could make some pictures and arrange some special things she'd like.'

The idea clearly struck a chord. Caity beamed as she went in search of a trowel and bucket, Lily padding faithfully at her heels.

Once she was out of earshot, Shelby glanced at Nathan, hoping she hadn't inadvertently intruded on his private feelings for his wife. 'You don't mind?'

'Not a bit. It's a brilliant idea. Caity's happy. By the way, I suggest we have that talk straight after dinner. Suit you?'

'Yes, please.' Although a nervous quiver struck her. What if, instead of clearing the way for a proper relationship with Nathan, she was laying down an ultimatum?

* * *

Nathan guessed Shelby would want to talk about work. Losing her job hadn't seemed to upset her all that much, but he was aware her finances were stretched. It wasn't his place to offer her money, apart from the wage they'd agreed on for child care. She would probably take offence. She was an independent woman for all her gentle ways. He could still hear her voice, that first day at the clinic, challenging him to prove his identity.

He was ready for their promised talk straight after dinner. They were doing the dishes while his daughter watched an episode of Peppa Pig on television.

'I guess you're thinking about your next job?' he opened. 'I've got a couple of ideas to run past you.'

She was slow to respond. 'Job?' She almost seemed confused.

While he was belting nails into Lexi's coop, he'd had a brilliant thought. Lexi wanted to open a riding school for the disabled, but that was far too big a project for her to take on by herself. Both he and Shelby were experienced at handling animals. The upheaval at the clinic could be the nudge to run their own business, incorporating Lexi in the scheme of things. The tea towel hanging forgotten in his hand, he began to lay out the idea but Shelby just shook the soapsuds off her hands and interrupted.

'I think we should sit down somewhere quiet. There're other things I want to talk about.'

Why didn't she come out and say what she meant? All this talk about talking was making him confused!

'What other things?'

'Can't you wait?' She sounded exasperated.

He began to laugh. 'What's the mystery? Spit it out! I'm all ears.'

'Why do you wear a wedding ring?' she blurted, as though it was a crime. This was the last thing he'd expected her to bring up, but if that's what she wanted . . .

'I don't know. I didn't think to take it off.'

'A gold ring on your fourth finger says you're married, Nathan.'

'I was married.'

'Exactly. Past tense. Every time I see you twist that ring, I know you're thinking of Samantha.'

Now he was getting an inkling of what this was about. Wedding rings, long talks — hell, this was rushing things. The last thing he wanted to do was hurt her. She was doing a brilliant job with Caity, she was easy on the eyes, and she'd given him sensual pleasure that kept him awake, reliving the one night they'd spent together. But if she wanted a proposal, he simply wasn't ready.

Best to pretend he didn't understand her. 'You keep saying you want to talk. Well, so do I. Don't you think my idea about a joint riding school plus vet clinic might have merit? You could even do your puppy training.'

Shelby pulled the tea towel from his hands.

'I want us to sit down together and talk about where we're going. If anywhere.'

'Going?' He wasn't aware they were going anywhere. 'You want to take a trip?'

'Well, that's one thing I want to talk about.'

More talk! Would she ever come to the point? Rubbing a hand over the stubble on his jaw, he shook his head.

'Shelby, I'm confused. I thought we were getting along pretty well. But if you've planned some trip, count me out. I've got too much to sort out.'

'The trip wouldn't be with you.'

'I see. Not with me.' He'd had enough of this beating round the bush. Was it a female thing? Samantha used to be the same, arranging trips, expecting him to drop everything and follow like a puppy dog. The fatigue and disappointment he was feeling made him frown.

'Look, I'm tired. Here's a suggestion. See if Lexi would babysit tomorrow and I'll take you out to dinner. We can relax and talk all you like then. How does that sound?'

'I'd like that. I'll see if Lexi's free.'

He was relieved. Pursuing any discussion tonight was likely to end in an argument, and the last thing he wanted was conflict. It was hard enough keeping his hands off Shelby in that soft, clingy sweater she was wearing. She was just a few steps away, settled back on the couch. Clenching his hands he stood up.

'If we've had our talk, I'm going to have a hot shower and an early night.'

Women were a mystery. Perhaps it was something to do with the moon. Before he weakened, he walked away.

* * *

Caity was ready to start the memory garden first thing next morning. She carefully searched the yard, considering likely sites, and decided on the space outside her bedroom window.

'I can talk to Mummy when I go to bed.'

The project involved serious planning. By morning tea time, the ground was weeded and dug over, and a border of river stones edged the small plot.

'What do we put in it?' The activity had brought a wild-rose flush to Caity's cheeks.

'What do you think Mummy would like?'

Caity considered. 'Flowers. Pretty clothes. A big chocolate cake. A picture of me and Daddy and Rusty.'

'Who's Rusty?'

'Mummy's horse.'

Caity spent the next hour thumbing through old magazines and choosing images of assertive, well-dressed models. As Shelby helped cut out pictures of summery dresses and jeans, she was forming a mental image of Samantha. Nathan's wife must have been a beautiful woman, active and yet domesticated. A farming article showed a chestnut horse ridden by a pretty woman wearing an Akubra hat. The old cookbook yielded a photo of an exotic Black Forest cake. Shelby queried the travel brochure showing happy tourists boarding a lavish cruise liner.

'What does this mean?'

'Mummy went away on a long trip all around the world.'

'And what about this picture?'

'She came back. Then she was a bird. So she flew up in the sky.'

Shelby looked at the image of soaring pigeons, their fluted wings translucent in the sunlight.

'I think these are lovely pictures,' she said softly. 'Let's go and find a box to put them in.'

Absorbed in her assignment, Caity hunted the garden for flowers, but the offerings of late winter were sparse. She returned disgruntled, carrying only a few storm-lashed blooms and a handful of wilting wattle blossom.

'They're old!' she complained, trying to stand the drooping bouquet in the small vase Shelby had brought in her luggage.

'I know the wattle flowers are dying.

But Caity, look at all these seeds! They're full of life and some of them will grow into new ones. Now what else do we need?'

'A picture of me. And Daddy.' She was thoughtful. 'And Lily. And Skip. And you.'

'All of us?'

Caity nodded.

'Everybody all together. My old mummy and my new one.'

This was awkward. Caity was starting to reconcile her loss, but Shelby could not deceive her. Nathan had made it very plain she could forget any hopes that he cared for her. Whenever she tried to raise that topic, he slithered away, as wary as a red-bellied snake. Overnight she had come to a decision. She had to accept that sooner or later they would all move on, going separate ways. And from his attitude last night, the indications were sooner rather than later. All she could do was to try and prepare Caity for that day, not lead her astray.

‘I’m not your new mummy, Caity,’ she said gently, crouching down beside the child.

‘But I want you to be!’ Caity flung her arms around Shelby, hugging her fiercely. ‘Daddy can make a picture of us all.’

‘Daddy doesn’t want to make that one. We’ll ask him for a different photo instead. Come on, let’s go and draw Lily and Skip. Mummy will like that picture.’

Fortunately small children were easily distracted. She wished her own emotions were as flexible. Compared to Samantha, she must be second-best. No wonder Nathan kept backing off. How could she compare?

However, he’d proposed a dinner date. After lunch she and Caity walked over to visit Lexi. Shelby hoped she could babysit, and wanted to see how Blade had adapted to his new environment. As soon as the clean-up was done, she planned to take the horse for a good ride. Thinking of the last time she'd cantered along the beach, her memories of Nathan and that fateful day sprang to mind. What a transition, from that hooded stranger to the confused man she lived with now! Perhaps everybody kept their real selves hidden. Yet the times she'd felt closest to Nathan weren't heroic. His coldness had made her angry. He'd shown unhappiness, and she'd longed to comfort him. He'd desired her, and somehow broken through her own fears of men. Was that intimacy?

When she reached the house, the old man was nowhere in sight. Leaving Caity to play with the kittens, she knocked.

'I'm in the bedroom! Come in.'

Lexi was helping Ông Ngoai out of bed and fitting on his slippers. He coughed faintly, as though he hadn't the strength to clear his lungs.

'Can you support his left side? He had a fall yesterday. I don't think anything's broken, but he's very shaken. He wants to use the bathroom.'

Shelby was glad to be useful. The full-time care of an aged person must be tiring. When the debilitated old man was safely back in bed, she readily accepted Lexi's invitation to stay a while. The events of the storm had changed their relationship from neighbors to friends and confidantes.

'You look worn out,' Shelby said, making no mention of the reason for her visit.

Clearly her friend was in no position to babysit. 'Can I help?'

Lexi held out her palms in a gesture of overload.

'I really need to go to the shops for groceries, but I'm worried about leaving Ông Ngoai. He's stubborn and quite likely to decide he'll get dressed and go and check the property.'

'That's easily solved. I'm going in to Maitland later. Give me your shopping list and I'll pick up what you need. What else is on your mind?'

'The horses need grooming and exercise. Nathan rebuilt the hen-house but that pesky rooster's still on the loose. I ought to look for him.'

'Surely we can help? Nathan's gone back to work today, but Caity and I are free.'

'He's a good man. I'm no relation, just a stranger, but he offered help.'

Shelby felt oddly proud of him. Nathan would go out of his way to help anyone in trouble.

'I can check the horses for you now. Has Blade settled?'

'He needs exercise. He's not like some of the other poor old nags. They can only manage a ramble.'

'Nathan mentioned your idea of a riding school for the disabled. Old horses would be ideal for that.'

Lexi just smiled. 'It's a dream, that's all. I couldn't take on such a project on my own. My hands are full with this one.' She nodded toward her grandfather, who did look very frail today. 'Was there any special reason for the visit, Shelby?'

'Just checking you're okay.' She couldn't possibly expect Lexi to babysit, under the circumstances. She and Nathan would just have to sit down and have their talk at home. Since he'd mentioned he was concerned about his parents, she wondered if he could be planning to pack up and go home to New Zealand. Anything might happen. His work situation was in flux and he had the added pressure of providing for Caity.

Wanting to clear her head, she headed out into the paddocks. Caity followed, carrying the wicker basket Lexi handed to her. While she scampered about, searching for stray hens and hidden eggs, Shelby found Blade, who whickered softly and pushed his soft nose against her shoulder as though he remembered her. The thought of the near-tragedy they'd been through together sent a shiver through her body.

'Poor old boy. Are you missing Jasmine?'

He bobbed his head, his dark eye alert as he nuzzled her again

'I know! I miss her too.' She'd only had one text message from her friend, with no mention of a return date.

She stayed with the horse, stroking his neck and talking to him as though he was a wise counselor. Friends came and went. If Nathan decided to go his separate way, she couldn't force him to change his mind. She still had the option of taking up her parents' offer. She knew her father well enough to predict he would not crumple even if his diagnosis was poor. He'd carry on as normal, and expect his family to support his decision. And in that case, turning down a free ticket to London would be crazy.

* * *

It was time to contact home and see what was going on. She settled Caity for an afternoon sleep and phoned her father. As usual, he adopted the affectionate, indulgent tone that reminded her he still saw her as his little girl. When she said she would come to a decision about the trip within a few days, he seemed surprised.

'What's the delay? Surely you wouldn't pass up the opportunity to see London?' He was a persuasive man. 'Wouldn't you like to see the Tate, Buckingham Palace, the Changing of the Guards?'

'Of course I'd love that. There's no mystery, Dad. I just have various commitments I need to sort out with someone.'

'Someone? Must be quite a special someone?'

He was fishing but she preferred to keep her attachment to Nathan and Caity private. Andrew continued to rattle off highlights of the proposed holiday. 'The Louvre, the Eiffel Tower, Monet's garden . . . '

When he used that cajoling tone she was ready to capitulate. Knowing her lavish father, she could expect luxury accommodation and tours that would illuminate the architecture, history and art of cities she'd only read about — not to mention all the spending money a tourist would be tempted to outlay. Only the thought of Nathan stopped her. He deserved to be consulted. Her absence would only add to his dilemmas. At the same time her father's next comment struck a chord.

'Anybody who's a real friend won't ask you to give up a chance like this. You should think about that, honey.'

He felt he could be honest. So could she.

'Have your test results come back, Daddy?'

There was a pause. 'So your mother's been babbling on.'

'Hardly babble. She told me about the melanoma, yes.'

'The doctor removed it. End of story.'

'And the second biopsy's clear?'

'A formality. I'll hear tomorrow. These chaps like to cover every base.'

It was wise to be thorough, where cancer was concerned. Andrew sounded in denial though with luck he would be proved right. There would be no spread into the lymph nodes and bloodstream, and he would be declared a healthy man. For the first time in her life, Shelby felt protective toward him. He was like a little boy, shaking his fist at ghosts under the bed.

'I hope it's good news,' she said softly. 'And I'll definitely let you know about the holiday soon.'

She sent Nathan a quick text, telling him about the change of plan. There was no need to cancel the dinner with him. She could prepare a special meal at home. She had to know his feelings. There were moments when their eyes met and he seemed so close to holding her. Then he simply turned and strode away. Their talk was long overdue.

Caity was still asleep. She didn't want a restless child ruining the evening, so gently woke her and said the dogs wanted a game. Caity lay blinking and rubbing her eyes, then held up her arms in a trusting gesture. The sweet girl was trying so hard to believe she belonged in a permanent, secure family again.

Skip was a ball chaser, and loved to

race up and down the yard until he collapsed in the dirt, panting, his long tongue hanging out. Lily preferred more sedate exercise. Her coat was starting to thicken and she'd lost the look of neglect. She was patient with Caity's attentions, seeming to understand the little girl meant no harm when she wrapped the dog in blankets and dragged her around the yard in an ancient go-cart she'd found in the back shed.

Now Skip was showing off, spinning and circling as though he felt free to be as silly as he liked. His high-pitched yelps blended with the chime of birds and the raucous laughter of a kookaburra. Reluctantly Shelby turned her mind to the evening ahead. Her stomach cramped with apprehension as she imagined the worst outcome; packing her bags and saying goodbye to Caity, the animals and the man she'd fallen in love with. Setting aside this negative picture, she quickly tidied the little girl and scribbled her own shopping list. She would do her very best to present an appetizing meal.

By the time she'd done her own shopping, located Lexi's groceries, and bought Caity a new book, she was running behind schedule. Revising her plans, she decided to settle for a stir-fry and an elaborate gateau she'd seen in the cake shop window. She made a brief detour to Lexi's house, then hurried home to feed and bathe Caity and have her settled early. She had the dinner to organize, and wanted plenty of time to dress and put on make-up for a change. Nathan had only seen her in her clinic uniform or the jeans and sweaters that suited a country lifestyle. Tonight she intended to look her best, as if they were eating in style.

* * *

Nathan stepped out of the Patrol and stood rooted to the ground as Shelby appeared in the doorway and waved. The electric-blue sheath dress hugged her slender curves, and the high heels of her matching shoes added height and grace to her appearance. Dark red lipstick defined her soft mouth and set off her creamy complexion, and the black eye liner and mascara intensified her hypnotic blue eyes.

'You look stunning!' The spontaneous words escaped him as he came close and caught the heady aroma of her warm, spicy perfume. This alluring woman eyed him with a faint smile, as though she could read his mind.

'We said we'd make it a special night.'

He grinned. 'Looks that way. Lexi couldn't show?'

'Her grandfather isn't well. But I promise we'll have just as good a time at home.'

He believed her. The house was warm, with a fire glowing in the hearth, and the table looked inviting. His daughter was nowhere to be seen. 'Where's Caity?'

'In bed. We have an agreement. She's

gone to bed with a new picture book, and tomorrow we're going to finish the memory garden.'

'Excellent. I'll read her a story and say goodnight to her now.'

And after that he needed to shower, shave and find something presentable to wear. Shelby had gone out of her way for him. The least he could do was try to be the escort she deserved. His dinner suit was back in Queensland but fortunately he'd chucked in his leather jacket and a few decent shirts and pants when he moved. Leaving Caity to her book and Shelby to her cooking, he unearthed his aftershave and headed to the bathroom.

He wouldn't have cared if the meal had consisted of peanut butter sandwiches, but Shelby was as good as her word. She'd bought a decent red wine to go with the beef stir-fry and served crisp rolls warm from the oven. In all the months since Samantha's death, he'd grown accustomed to eating alone or on the run, existing on takeaways or greasy counter meals swallowed in a noisy atmosphere of Sky TV or rackety band music. Shelby had brought back some sense of family to meal time, though that was often disrupted by Caity's finicky ways. With Shelby's care, he had to admit his daughter had improved remarkably in that regard.

Now he realized how relaxing it was to sit down as adults, enjoying each other's company as much as the satisfying mouthfuls of food. The firelight cast lustrous highlights on Shelby's dark hair and glinted on her silver earrings. The matching pendant seemed to direct his eye to the cleavage framed by her plunging neckline. Her gaze met his and he saw warmth and curiosity, as though he was a painting whose meaning she was determined to fathom.

Still, she seemed in no hurry to raise whatever personal issue she wanted to talk about.

'How's the clinic merger going?' she asked. Although she had resigned, she retained an interest in his work and the changes underway.

'The new part-owner introduced himself to us today. He's in the process of moving his family to the city.' Nathan drained his glass. He rarely drank, but the wine went well with the tasty food. Shelby had gone to a lot of trouble for him tonight. 'He has kids in secondary school and prefers the options here. They're still working out details for staffing both clinics. Nobody seems quite sure what the new allocation of duties will be.'

'We know they don't include me, for a start!' Shelby paused. 'However, I do have other options.'

'Are you going to share them?' He was surprised she'd already formed some other plan. Tonight he hoped to talk to her about the idea he'd formed after his conversation with Lexi. The more he'd thought about it, the wider the possibilities seemed. As a trio, with pooled skills and assets, they could consider veterinary services, breeding, boarding kennels and Lexi's own dream of a riding school for the disabled.

But first he'd have to get his mind on practical matters. It was hard to focus while Shelby was leaning toward him, her expression asking him to understand. Now what problem was she about to raise? She held his gaze, so tantalizingly close he had to lean back in his chair to protect himself from melting under her spell. This was where he had to choose. The past with Samantha or the future with Shelby. There would be no going back once he followed his instincts and allowed passion to overrule caution.

'My parents have made me a very generous offer,' she was saying. 'They want to give me a trip to Europe. And I've decided I'd be a fool to turn it down.'

9

What was she saying now?

'I need you to hear me out, Nathan.'

Her words whirled in his head. Her father. Cancer. Her mother. Panic attacks when she was a teenager. A duty now to prove she was healthy and available to her parents at a time of crisis . . .

As if to complicate a situation that sounded incomprehensible, there was an urgent knocking at the door. He leaped to his feet and strode out. This was the worst possible time to be interrupted and he would give the intruder short shrift. But it was Lexi who stood there in the dark, all her composure vanished. Something was very wrong. Tears choked her voice as her anxious words spilled out.

'My grandfather's wandered off and it's already dark. I've searched and called, but he's gone.'

Shelby had come to the door. 'Come inside. What happened? When did you notice he was gone?'

'I went to feed the hens and check the stables. I left him safe in his bed but when I went home he was gone. No coat, only his slippers. And he's so weak, he's sure to have fallen. If he stays out in the cold all night, he won't survive.'

'He had a fall yesterday,' Shelby murmured to Nathan. 'He's definitely not fit to be out at night.'

Lexi nodded. 'The last week I've noticed his mind's not quite right. He sometimes calls me by my mother's name. He even thinks he's back in Vietnam.'

'We'll find him.' Whatever needed to be said between himself and Shelby would just have to wait. How many more times would he have reason to leave her standing there, thinking her own thoughts and presuming he didn't care? But this was a real emergency and his trained mind clicked into gear. This wasn't the time for flowery words but on impulse he turned and pressed an urgent, inarticulate kiss on Shelby's warm lips. 'You stay here with Caity. Lexi and I will search.'

'Yes, go. Find him. I'll stoke up the fire. Nathan . . . ?' Her hand was warm as she pressed his. 'Thank you for helping.'

Lexi held out a tattered shawl. 'This was dropped on the ground, just outside the house. He usually rests this over his knees.'

Nathan grabbed his keys and whistled for Skip, showing him the piece of blanket.

'We'll take him along. He's not a tracking dog, but he might be able to pick up the scent. We'll go in my vehicle, Lexi. Don't worry. We'll find the old man. He'll soon be back in bed.'

The four wheel drive bumped and bounced over the rough, rain-sodden terrain. Heavy clouds swept across the sky, dimming the moon, and tree branches tossed, the sounds of their rustling foliage strangely sinister. Nathan pulled up and turned to Lexi, who huddled beside him, peering out at the shadows.

'Any idea which way he might have gone? A favorite part of the land?'

'He's been fussing about the bee hives. They're in that hollow, over near the creek . . . '

She fell silent as he read her thoughts, remembering his own dread when he realized Caity had wandered toward the water just a few days before.

'I can't take the vehicle that way, not with fences. We'd better get out and walk. Has the overflow drained yet?'

'We still have shallow water lying in the low spots. Nothing more than ankle-deep.'

'Go slowly then. Even shallow water can conceal hazards. We'll stay together as it's dark.'

Although they both carried flashlights, the batteries would only last for a limited time. It would be no fun to wade through mud in the darkness. In silence the pair tramped cautiously in the direction of the hives. Skip, enjoying this impromptu outing, raced ahead.

The hives were dim shapes now. Surely nobody would attempt to relocate such heavy, bulky objects, but by the sound of Lexi's words, her grandfather was showing signs of dementia.

'Ông Ngoai!' Lexi repeatedly called his name but there was no response. Nathan whistled the dog and held the blanket to his nose. Skip just barked expectantly, as though asking for a ball game.

'I'm afraid we're playing to an empty theatre. He doesn't understand.'

They traipsed ahead, checking the ground as they passed the hives, but there was no sign of the old man.

'Not here. Which way now? Did he ever go near the creek?' Even saying the words filled him with dread. Not another drowning! Had his Jonah curse spread to his neighbors?

'He hasn't been here for years. But who knows what's in his mind these days?'

Lexi flashed the pale beam of light across the surface of the creek. 'I can't see anything!' She sounded despairing. 'He's gone. Wherever he is, the cold will kill him.'

Just then Skip's shrill bark of excitement caught their attention. Trailing their fingers in the barely visible flow, willows along the bank formed a canopy where the dog had disappeared. Nathan pushed the drooping leaves aside, revealing a still figure huddled on its side. Lexi screamed. 'He's dead!'

'Hang on. We don't know that.' Nathan gently eased the dog aside and felt the inert wrist for a pulse.

'It's weak, and he's unconscious, but he's alive.'

With a sob of relief, Lexi threw herself down beside her grandfather, stripping off her parka and laying it over his cold form. In turn, Nathan shed his leather jacket.

'Wear this. I'll be warm enough, carrying him.'

Nathan briefly wondered about the

wisdom of moving Ông Ngoai in case of spinal injury; but leaving him to the mercy of the water and the wind wasn't an option. Lexi led the way back to the vehicle, Skip bounding ahead as though this was a delightful game.

Nathan was pushing his strength to its limits as he tripped and stumbled on invisible obstacles. Though his burden was thin and wasted, the old man was a dead weight, and every muscle was screaming by the time they reached his vehicle.

'We'll take him to my place,' he said, forestalling Lexi who assumed her grandfather should be at home. 'I'm no physician, but I do have enough training to see him through the night and get him to hospital if need be.' Privately he was concerned about hypothermia and shock.

'I can't leave him.' She was distraught. 'If he wakes . . . He speaks no English.'

'Of course. You must come too.'

'I'll go and pack.'

'There's no time, Lexi. We must get your grandfather warmed up and see what condition he's in. Hop in. We'll lend you whatever you need.'

There was a faint murmur of pain from the old man as he was loaded into the vehicle. Investigations would have to wait. Lexi and Skip scrambled aboard and the group headed home.

* * *

The house had never seemed so inviting as when they stepped into the warm, brightly-lit atmosphere. Shelby had been busy making preparations for their return. A good fire crackled and she had blankets and pillows already waiting on the chesterfield.

'I think we'll lay him on the floor,' Nathan suggested, keeping to himself the possibility that, if Ông Ngoai went into cardiac arrest, he would be in a better resuscitation position. 'Just spread that doona near the hearth. We'll have to get his clothes off and wrap him up warmly.'

He did not want to alarm Lexi, but quite frankly he was not expecting a good outcome. A fit man of Nathan's age could well shake off the symptoms of such an experience, but it was demanding too much of a frail, elderly body. All he could do was keep a watchful eye.

While Lexi sat guarding the still form, Shelby drew Nathan aside.

'Should we move some mattresses into the room?'

Nathan shook his head.

'Don't worry about it. I don't think anyone's going to get much sleep tonight.'

'Shouldn't he go to hospital?'

'I've decided against it for now. The shock of moving him to a foreign environment would do more harm than risking things here. I'll watch him.'

'Are you sure? You look beat.' She reached up and stroked a lock of wet hair from his forehead. 'What can I do?'

'Heat towels and blankets. We'll warm up the central torso first. Lexi's on hand to reassure him, in case he wakes.'

'It's a miracle you found him at all.'

'It was Skip. The old man was under the willow canopy. We would have missed him in the dark.'

'What are his chances?'

Nathan's shrug told her not to be too hopeful. His prediction of a wakeful night was right. However, within an hour, Ông Ngoai showed signs of consciousness returning and was able to convey to Lexi that he had pain in his left wrist. Presumably he'd stumbled and put out his hand to break the fall. Nathan decided it was likely the injury was just a bad sprain but that could be assessed when the patient was checked next day at the hospital.

In the morning, the house had the air of narrowly-averted crisis, with bedding strewn everywhere and its inhabitants bleary-eyed and yawning. Only the dogs and Caity assumed everything was normal, the animals lining up for their breakfast and Caity demanding to know when she could finish work on the memory garden. Nathan phoned the clinic and left a message to say he would not be in until the afternoon. Between them, he and Lexi arranged to transport her grandfather to Emergency for a precautionary checkup and X-ray.

'You are true friends,' was Lexi's parting comment, when Shelby offered to see to the horses and the hens while she was away. 'Your good deed will be returned to you one day.' But the relief on Lexi's face as she scolded her grumbling runaway was quite enough reward.

Shelby put the house in order and took Caity over to the paddocks to attend to Lexi's animals. As she tramped back from the stables, she wondered how Lexi could continue to manage the care of her confused grandfather without help, although she could understand why she felt responsible. He'd brought his own cultural background with him to the new country when he emigrated from

Vietnam. The little English he'd picked up had been lost, he did not eat a Western diet, and his only link with reality was Lexi's input.

'I will care for him. I promised my mother,' was all Lexi would say, when Shelby had once asked her about placing him in a care facility. But if he was going to wander and risk injury, the problem would have to be faced.

Unaware that he was an accidental hero, Skip was waiting by the gate with Lily when they returned. The dogs demanded a ball game, and the glazier finally arrived to repair Shelby's window. It was nearing lunch time when Caity proudly carried her box of mementos out to the garden. The neat plot of ground with its edging of river stones was ready to receive the memories of the little girl. Carefully she opened the green metal safety box she'd chosen at the hardware store in town, and laid out her pictures in a line. Without tears, she placed a solemn kiss on the image she'd selected to represent Samantha, and placed it beside the other cut-out pictures she'd gathered.

'Is there anything else you want to put in the box before we bury it?'

The child shook her curls. Fortunately Caity seemed to have accepted that Shelby could not step in and make a replacement family with Nathan.

'I want nice flowers.'

Shelby had to agree — the bedraggled wattle had seen better days. There was just nothing bright or colorful in the garden at this time of year.

As if in answer to the problem, Nathan arrived back from the hospital and walked over to the garden. He was carrying daffodils; big yellow trumpets with golden centers, which he offered to Shelby with a warm expression.

'They're gorgeous!' It was the first time a man had given her flowers. But Caity deserved them more today. 'See what Daddy's brought!'

Caity's face lit up and Shelby murmured to Nathan, 'That was timely. Caity is taking all this very seriously.'

Nathan looked thoughtful as his daughter ran off to refresh the water in the vase. 'This garden is a fabulous idea. Poor little kid, she was left in a total vacuum. She wasn't taken to the funeral. Barbara felt she was too young. So one day Samantha was there and everything was normal. And the next, she disappeared.'

In a way, he was talking about himself. The wrench had been so sudden, surreal in fact. Sure, there'd been an argument and words exchanged. But he'd fully intended to patch things up with Sam. If she'd really planned to pack her bags and leave him, as Barbara implied, she'd certainly succeeded.

This act of making a memorial was tangible. It was time to let Samantha rest, and get on with life. 'There's one thing I'd like to add.'

Shelby looked at him, inquiring, as he eased the gold ring from his finger and dropped it into the box.

'This belongs with Caity's memories.'

'Nathan, are you sure?'

She knew the act was symbolic as he held out his hand to her, palm-up, in such a gesture of surrender that she felt a strange hesitation. He just nodded. 'I'm quite sure.'

The moment was interrupted as Caity crouched to arrange the daffodils.

'We can bury the box now.' She sounded worried. 'But what if it rains?'

'How about I build a little roof over the garden?' Nathan picked up the spade and prepared a hole to receive Caity's memories of her mother. The plot was finally finished, and in the way of children she patted down the earth and stood up, satisfied to move on to the next distraction.

'I'm hungry, Daddy!'

'Let's find some lunch then, before I have to go to work.'

Nathan hoisted her onto his shoulders and carried her inside. Shelby followed. His gesture with the ring had been startling. So he was ready to move forward? Was she? Shelby was actually relieved when he left for work. She'd kept up every day chat, using it like a shield to hold away the meaning of what he'd done. There was only one possible explanation for the flowers, the ring, and most of all the way his gaze had been so frank and open as he'd offered her his hand. It was as good as a proposal — oh, not a marriage proposal, but an invitation to join him as a partner and, yes, a lover.

Who was this man who'd appeared so suddenly in her life and turned it upside down? Nathan Monroe, a strong, decisive man in his prime, a man of worldly experience. He was a qualified vet, a landowner, a man who'd been married, weathered the complex ups and downs of that state, and fathered a child. The sheer weight of his experience stood in contrast to Shelby's own life. She'd barely left home and broken away from her parents' support. She'd suffered panic attacks and dealt with fears that had no basis now in reality. She was simply over-sensitive. Hadn't Trevor known it, and told her she needed to toughen up? Even Jasmine used to remind her she was too soft, and ready to fall for any sob story. They were right. She was too open to the raw pain of suffering and loss. Perhaps that was how she was able to help Caity, but what use was it to a man like Nathan?

She had nothing to give him and she knew it. There was a good reason for the picture Caity had selected to represent her mother. It was an image of a laughing, confident woman astride a chestnut horse, her mane of thick hair blowing as she rode into the wind. How could Shelby possibly compare with that lithe, sexual woman, when she was virtually still a virgin? The near-rape of her teenage years had imprinted images of brutality and violence on her mind, while that one-off, clumsy encounter with Jason hardly qualified as love-making. No wonder she'd never gone down that road again with him.

She must have been deluded, fanta-sizing about Nathan! They'd spent exactly one night in bed, with a small child ensuring they couldn't explore any further than stroking and gentle caresses. Had she liked that? Oh yes! But no red-blooded man was going to be happy with cuddles for the rest of his life.

She was damaged goods and she had to get away, before Nathan put his heart on the line and got hurt all over again. And she knew how she had to make that happen. Slowly she picked up the phone and telephoned her parents. Andrew would have his results by now, but whether or not the melanoma had been completely excised, she'd made up her mind. If the trip was still on, she would go. She had to put space between herself and Nathan. They were on the verge of massive change. Before he made his move irrevocably, she had to let go, and leave Caity and her father to rebuild their lives without her.

Andrew's tests had cleared him of the melanoma, and her parents' delight when she asked them to book her fare was touching. Why didn't she feel the slightest bit elated? It didn't matter. She was doing the right thing. Now she just had to break the news to Nathan.

* * *

Usually he came home to a warm house and the appetizing aromas of food cooking. Last night's events must have taken their toll. Shelby sat huddled on the chesterfield beside the ashes of the dead fire.

'Everything okay?'

'Yes. My window's fixed. I've moved my stuff back into the bedroom.'

'Did you hear from Lexi?' She looked so sad. Had the old man suffered some setback? Earlier, the hospital had cleared him as fit to return home with Lexi.

'Yes. She brought me up to speed. Her grandfather's a tough old man. Doesn't want to take his medicine!'

'Antibiotics. The hospital found he has a urinary infection. That can cause confusion in elderly people.'

'Really?'

She sounded completely flat. 'Feeling under the weather?' He laid a sympathetic hand on her shoulder and at once she leapt to her feet as though she had a hundred things to see to. The least he could do was relieve her of cooking a meal.

'Why don't we all pile in the vehicle and I'll treat us to takeout? I reckon Skip deserves a hamburger, after last night. What do you say?'

'I'm not hungry. There's soup and toast.' Already she was heading to the kitchen and putting out plates and spoons as though her life depended on it.

'If you like.' Soup and toast weren't the issue, that much was obvious. 'By the way, I thought we might have that talk tonight?' Perhaps that was why she seemed so off-hand. After all, she'd been at him about it for days. She could hardly blame him for last night's interruption. In a way, he was glad of it, because he'd had time to decide what he wanted.

'I'm tired, Nathan. I think I'll just have an early night.'

Why was she giving him the brush-off like this? He placed his hands on her shoulders, turning her round to face him, but even so, her eyes were down-cast and her mouth was set.

'What's the matter?'

She tried to pull away but he pinned her with his arms, letting his hands slide past her ribcage to span her slender waist. 'Come on, Shelby. Tell me what's wrong.'

Suddenly she was fighting him, tearing herself free as though he was a captor. 'Don't, Nathan!'

He stepped back as though burnt. 'I'm sorry. I didn't mean to upset you.'

'I have to get on with cooking. Can you get Caity? She's outside with Lily.'

He had absolutely no idea what was going on. Women! What was that damn book Samantha had wanted him to read? Men are from Mars, Women are from Venus? Shelby was definitely in Venus mode tonight, and his irritation was building to Martian levels. With a real effort he pulled himself into line. Shelby had every reason to be tired and moody, after the night they'd had with the neighbors.

They ate in silence. After the sparse meal, he offered to clean up. 'I'll run you a bath,' he suggested, hastily adding, 'if you like.' She nodded. At least he'd got something right tonight.

She left him and he washed up, his mind picturing her slender body stretched out under the warm water. That tough, defensive female pushing past him in the kitchen wasn't the real Shelby. He could remember the tender longing she'd aroused in him, that day of the beach rescue, as he watched her sleeping. With her lips softly parted and the curve of sooty eyelashes resting on her flushed cheeks, she'd looked virginal, untouched.

He'd certainly done nothing to take advantage of her. Could that be the problem? They were a man and a woman living like brother and sister when obviously they weren't. He'd kept his horny urges under wraps, knowing that while Samantha filled his memories, he would have been taking advantage of Shelby, or anyone else.

Now his daughter had shown him it was time to let go. Thanks to Shelby, Caity's loss had been put to rest outside, in her memory garden. And so was his. He'd put away his wedding ring and his marriage out there in the peaceful plot of ground. That time of his life was past. This was Shelby's time, if he could persuade her.

He settled Caity in bed and read her a story. As he walked back along the hall, Shelby emerged from the bathroom. Flushed and scented, she brushed past him, a white towel draped around her. So tempting. One little tug and . . .

'Daddy!' Caity sounded imperious. 'You forgot to say goodnight to Lily.'

By the time he'd patted the swaddled dog, Shelby had gone to her own room and the door was firmly closed. Well, he could wait. First thing tomorrow, he would hand in his notice. The terms of his employment had changed. He didn't care for the off-hand treatment of Shelby, and to tell the truth he wasn't deriving much satisfaction from the routine clinic duties. Trevor wouldn't be unduly concerned. As a locum, it was likely Nathan was on the cull list too.

His mind buzzed with ideas. Sitting with Lexi at the hospital, he'd listened to her dream of starting up a riding school for disabled children. The idea stirred widening circles of potential. Why not include veterinary services, pet boarding and grooming . . . ? Shelby had excellent skills with animals, Lexi had the land and horses, and he had the money and the training to set up first class facilities. The three of them could pool resources and run their own business. Tomorrow he would put his proposal to Shelby and test her reaction. Just a few short weeks ago, his life had felt like a salvage operation after horrendous trauma. Happiness wasn't on the radar. Now he had a home, his daughter, pets. How Shelby felt, he didn't know. Would she consider joining forces? He needed to stop procrastinating and simply tell her he was falling in love with her. She'd probably flip. He'd done nothing but push her away, avoid all her hints, take her help for granted.

He was surprised when she walked into the room, fully dressed.

'I thought you'd gone to have an early night.' He lifted the stylus off the lyrical duet from La Traviata.

'I need to explain something,' she said, and for some reason he guessed bad news was coming.

Surely he must be hearing wrong. She was talking about some trip to Europe. Had she ever mentioned it before? When had this bombshell occurred? While he'd been on the roof, of course, or fixing that damned chicken coop for the neighbor. He'd had his chance. Plenty of them. All that talk he'd taken as female dither, all the turn-offs he'd adopted, making sure she wasn't pushing him into something he wasn't ready for . . . Serve him right! He'd been too successful. He'd left it too late and Shelby was about to walk out of his life.

And Caity's. A stab of pain gutted him at the thought of what he'd done to his daughter. It was so obvious she liked Shelby. That memorial garden thing, the cooking, the way Shelby used the dogs to model behaviors Caity was resistant to . . . He simply had to convince this beautiful girl that Caity needed her, the dogs needed her, hell, he needed her.

Europe be damned. Could he change her mind?

'I don't understand. What about Caity? The dogs?'

* * *

Deliberately, Shelby switched off the center light, leaving the room lit only by the fireplace, where a large log had burned down to a gentle glow. She had to tell Nathan the truth. At whatever cost to their relationship, she knew it was time to be honest and open, though the thought of airing her most private fears was devastating. She was about to drive Nathan away. Her hands clenched and her breathing felt heavy and irregular. When she spoke, the words were slow and halting. She began to lay out the facts, like disastrous hands of playing cards. She told him about the teenage trauma, how foolishly she'd acted in accepting a joyride with a group of boys. She told him she'd been ill for years, suffering panic attacks, dependent on her parents, not able to step out into the world. She was stupid, gullible. Didn't the Internet scam she'd fallen for last year prove that? She'd lost all her savings, over a thousand dollars, thinking she was helping pay for treatment of a terminally ill child in Africa. A scam. She'd found out only when her money ran out and the communications changed, became hostile, even threatening. There was no child; just a band of professional thieves, skilled in extortion and even brain-washing techniques.

The worst thing was still to come. How could any woman expect a man to understand she couldn't stand the thought of having sex? Her eyes cast down, she spoke so softly Nathan had to strain to hear what she was saying.

'When you put your arms around me tonight, I freaked out.'

He didn't say anything. He looked gutted, naturally. And she knew her negative feelings had nothing at all to do with Nathan. How could she convey to him that terrible, trapped feeling, hands holding her down, and leering faces leaning closer? Only the timely arrival of a police car that night had saved her and Jasmine from gang rape.

No, she would never be able to respond like a normal woman to the touches of her man. She shivered, imagining the heat and lust driving a rampant bull or stallion as he took his mate.

A dull thud startled her as the burning log disintegrated, shooting sparks up the chimney. The shadows in the room resettled. Shelby swallowed. Nathan still hadn't spoken. She had to tell him the rest.

'I just can't bear the thought of sex.'

Now he knew. At least she'd saved him from the declaration she knew he was ready to make. Whatever he wanted, she couldn't pretend. Oh, all these past days and nights as they'd slowly let down their defenses and found common ground, she'd tried to delude herself. There'd been moments. Casual touches, gazes that had met and held, one special night when she'd discovered the meaning of tenderness.

'Is that why you're leaving us?'

Surely it was enough! She half-smiled, even as tears spilled down her cheeks, and she explained about her father's melanoma.

'So it's quite a mixed bag of reasons? You want to travel, your parents are keen to give you this trip, and there won't be any sex on the other side of the world?'

His lighthearted remark shocked her. Surely he must be vastly relieved he hadn't got himself entangled with a neurotic, frigid woman? He actually seemed to be taking her problem in his stride.

'Are you laughing at me?' Her whole body was shivering with a thin, wiry vibration of nerves as the repressed traumas of long ago invaded her awareness. Her skin tingled and she felt dizzy.

Nathan held out his hand, again in that palm-up gesture.

'Miss Shelby Summers, I am not laughing at you. I'd love to get hold of the bastards who set this whole situation in motion, because I'd make sure they never troubled another woman ever again. However . . . ' He was patting the cushion beside him. 'Could you bring yourself to sit here beside me and tell me all about this holiday? Because it's a really wonderful opportunity and I think you'd be crazy to turn it down.'

A rush of love was starting in her toes and creeping up, right through her shaking, trembling body and lighting a warm glow in her heart. Complete acceptance. He didn't think she was a freak. He didn't intend to grab her and show her how much of a man he was. He just wanted to sit beside her. And that, to start with, felt exactly right. A small sob escaped her as she moved toward him. She sat down and stared ahead. 'I suppose you think I'm an idiot.'

In response he put a gentle arm around her shoulder. She let him cradle her, nestling her head against his chest. The steady thud of his heart was like a clock, striking out the past until all that was left was now. Once, Nathan eased away and set the stylus on the aria he'd been playing before she came into the room. Enfolding her again, he sat without moving while the glorious harmony of two voices in perfect tune poured out and surrounded them.

10

The surge of the jet was irresistible as the Australia-bound plane roared down the runway and angled skywards. Three weeks ago, on her first ever flight, Shelby had gripped her father's arm as the powerful machine climbed and she looked down on apparently solid clouds. Below that mirage had been her familiar world, where Nathan and Caity were driving homeward to resume their lives without her.

Naturally her father had booked business class tickets. As the seatbelt sign was turned off, other passengers began fitting headphones or checking out movie titles. But Shelby didn't want entertainment. She and Nathan had an unspoken pact. Her disclosure had brought them to an impasse, and this interlude apart would allow them both to decide whether they had a future together. Her parents had ordered drinks from the hostess but Shelby had declined, feeling as disoriented as though she'd been plucked from earth and deposited in some other dimension.

Now she was traveling home alone. Her mother's effort to attract an agent had been set back until the woman returned from her summer break in Spain. Andrew had simply extended their three-week holiday, booking accommodation on one of the luxury cruisers that followed the Seine to the Normandy coast. Though he was keen for Shelby to stay, she'd refused, telling her parents that although she'd had a wonderful trip, it was time for her to go home.

Without visible landmarks, she had no idea whether they were flying over land or water. There'd be a stopover in Singapore but she'd declined the suggestion she could have a few days to sightsee. Exotic destinations felt like delays.

She sat reflecting on the trip. Already her perception of time and distance had changed so much that Nathan seemed to be light years away. She'd arrived in a country where night was day and even the seasons were reversed. In mid-summer London, news readers waxed lyrical over warm temperatures and strolling citizens in summer clothing took advantage of the sunshine.

In his lavish way, Andrew had booked their accommodation at the Dorchester, where most of the patrons were in her parents' age bracket — wealthy people who made their expectations known. Elaborate afternoon teas and wine tastings were held in cloistered rooms with thick carpeting and servile waiters. Shelby kept her discomfort from her parents. A distance had crept in between them. She did not belong here. She was barely entering adulthood, while for them the creep of age and infirmity waited. Oh, perhaps not for decades, but Andrew's recent brush with cancer made him vulnerable. He seemed less powerful, less in control. Her mother sensed it, fussing over him, and confiding her fear of losing him to her daughter. In a partial reversal of roles, Shelby tried to reassure her.

'Mum, you needn't worry. The doctor says Dad will be fine.'

But even as she spoke, she knew no words could halt time.

Andrew had arranged tours of galleries and museums. On a visit to the London Eye, Shelby stood with her parents in the glass observation cage as it slowly revolved, her father pointing out Big Ben and London Bridge. In Paris, they visited the Louvre and the Jardin des Tuileries, walked beside the Seine and photographed the Arc de Triomphe. But all the while Shelby thought of Nathan. How much more all this would mean if he could be with her. She treasured their brief messages to each other, but what could you say in a text?

Quite simply, she was pining. Even the Parisian dogs, strutting with their owners, were reminders of Skip and Lily. She bought postcards of the Eiffel Tower, but what she remembered, as the plane seamlessly sewed up the miles, was the park near the monument, where an old-fashioned carousel revolved. She'd watched a young girl in a brass-buttoned navy jacket, her red skirt billowing out in the breeze as her father lifted her onto a painted pony. She'd gripped the barley-twist pole, and Shelby thought of the little girl back home who had captured her heart, and wished she could be there.

The rattle of the refreshment trolley recalled her from her memories. A hostess was making her way along the aisle, taking orders for drinks. On this return journey Shelby was traveling economy class; not caring about a night's discomfort. She just wanted the trip to be over. It felt like ruling a thick black line through the past and opening a new ledger.

Would he be waiting for her when she disembarked? He'd been incredibly understanding about her trauma, but in her heart she dreaded the moment when he faced reality. She'd know soon.

If he wasn't at the airport . . . Forcing her mind to the present, she ordered a glass of wine and stared without interest at the movie showing on the wide screen ahead. She'd seen it before — New in Town, a romantic comedy. Renee Zellweger was just breaking up with her boyfriend. Shelby hoped it wasn't a bad omen for her reunion with Nathan.

⋆ ⋆ ⋆

The traffic on the freeway had been crawling for the past twenty minutes.

Crouched motorcyclists zipped in and out of lanes like marauding hornets, and the hopeless procession of frustrated drivers vented their displeasure with toots and long blasts of the horn.

Nathan wondered whether there was a serious accident up ahead. The thought hardly improved his gloomy mood. This delay didn't augur well for his reunion with Shelby.

Two hours for the drive to the airport

should have aced it, but now it looked like he was going to be late.

Several kilometers further on, he saw the reason for the delay was roadwork. On a Saturday, when people were heading out of town? He gave an impatient groan as the road worker pointedly swung the sign from 'Slow' to 'Stop', while a seemingly endless procession of cars began to surge in the other direction.

Nathan switched off the ignition and sat tapping his foot and drumming his fingers on the steering wheel. The sun blazed down, heating the vehicle until he broke out in a sweat. He gave the dirty windscreen a blast of water and turned on the wipers. The outlook sharpened and he stared with displeasure at drab eucalypts lining both sides of the road, reddish foliage regenerating after last season's bush fires. The mournful croak of ravens sounded like a soundtrack for a Stephen King movie.

He'd lain awake most of the night, rehearsing what he had to say to Shelby. Even thinking about it increased the sick feeling in his gut. Because he wanted her in his life. Of that he was quite certain. They'd come together by chance and found they worked as a team. Caity adored her. Their mutual love of animals could lead to a business partnership, while on the domestic front she'd stepped in and filled the gaps in his life.

He'd hardly thought about sex since Samantha died. His body went into shut-down mode, and everything just stopped. But from the day he'd pulled Shelby's horse free and watched her sleeping, he'd begun to thaw. Whatever that connection could be called, he was sure she felt it too. She wasn't stiff and rejecting; quite the opposite. He was sure she'd felt desire, that stormy night they'd had to share a bed.

Since she'd confided in him, she'd been more affectionate, which merely made him more confused. The confession she'd made had filled him up with sadness. She'd said she couldn't stand the thought of sex. It would be pointless to walk into a situation, expecting her to change. Sometimes in his work he came across traumatized animals, too ingrained in fear or aggression to be rehabilitated. It was all very well for Shelby to look at him with that soft, admiring gaze, as though he was a hero. He was just an average guy with normal urges. Perhaps he'd given her the wrong idea about himself.

He wasn't a priest or holy man. If he did remarry, he wanted a woman who would love him and respond to him. And that wasn't going to happen with Shelby. Knowing what she'd told him, he had to ask himself if he was capable of that kind of sacrifice. And the honest answer was No.

The alternative felt just as bad. She might seem soft, but when she'd made up her mind she was no mild-mannered nanny. She'd stood up to her boss and she would do the same to him, if he called off their relationship. He could lay a bet she would pack up her bags and walk out of his life. And then what? He would probably hate himself. Had he thought it through? Was there any way they could live together, but not in the intimacy of marriage? Did it really matter? Come on! Who was he kidding? Of course it mattered! He wasn't even thirty, she was twenty-two. One day he'd like to think Caity might have a brother or sister.

The road worker swiveled the sign to allow Nathan's lane slow passage. He started the motor and eased forward, thinking he'd be lucky to make the airport by late afternoon. Fortunately, knowing Shelby would be jet-lagged, he'd left Caity and the dogs in Lexi's care for the night, and booked a two-bedroom motel accommodation. They could enjoy a meal and an early night before driving back to Newcastle in the morning. And he'd keep the dreaded talk to himself meanwhile. Perhaps a miracle would happen. Otherwise, he was dead in the water.

Thank God! The delay was left behind as drivers gained the speed limit and headed into the city.

* * *

Shelby was so sure Nathan would be waiting. A mob of strangers hung around the exit point as she emerged from Customs and scanned the crowd, searching for the one, familiar face. All around her, reunited families and children were hugging and kissing. She'd pinned her hopes on this moment, yet she was walking out alone. So, what had she expected? The Hollywood finale, with romantic music building as the lovers fell into each other's arms? She'd pushed him away, and he'd responded as any normal man would. Nathan was just getting over one disaster. Why would he walk straight into another with a neurotic woman?

Pride made her swallow the pain at the back of her throat. She felt weak, and stepped aside from the crowd, setting her suitcase down as though she needed a rest. People jostled her. Loud voices and squealing children jarred her nerves. She squeezed her eyelids shut, willing tears not to spill. No way would she stand in a public airport, bawling her eyes out. She would need to catch a taxi bus to get back to Newcastle. She'd get a coffee, settle down, then find the booking counter.

'Shelby!'

Relief rioted through her body as she saw him pushing through the crowd.

'I thought you weren't coming!' She didn't want to conceal her relief. It was time to let him see how much she'd missed him.

'I'm so sorry. There was a hold-up on the freeway.'

She simply gazed into his eyes, seeing uncertainty and hope.

'I've really missed you. So has Caity.'

'You didn't bring her?'

'She's at Lexi's, with the dogs. I thought we might stay in Sydney overnight. That is, if you want to?'

Her heart picked up pace as she guessed what he had in mind. Across that vast stretch of space, he must have sensed the change she'd undergone. She'd dropped her inhibitions and her fears like an out-of-season coat. Laying them out, voicing them to Nathan, had shown her she was ruled by shadows from the past. In reality she was a woman, and she was ready to admit she wanted a full life as a wife and mother — to Caity, now, and perhaps one day to a baby of her own. Of their own. As if denying the shy girlhood she'd retreated to, she'd even slipped her parents' attention and gone shopping for lacy lingerie in that Park Lane boutique. And apparently tonight she'd have a chance to flaunt it! Her eyes were misty with emotion as she reached out and slipped her small hand into Nathan's.

'That's a great idea, Nathan. And I've missed you, too.'

He gently detached his hand and picked up her suitcase. 'Let's grab a coffee. I had to skip lunch. How about you?'

'I don't know. What's the time?' She

was completely disoriented. Sitting up all night hadn't been fun. Her back hurt, her legs ached. But she was happy. She was home, and tonight she and Nathan were going to bed together.

As they drove to the motel, Shelby filled the silence with stories of her trip. Nathan seemed distracted — probably negotiating the unfamiliar route. He pulled the four wheel drive into a drab concrete parking lot and carried her bag toward the office to check in. The cheap atmosphere of plastic chairs and faded silk flowers was matched by the boredom of the receptionist, who tossed over the keys and went on with her cell phone texting.

'Hardly the Dorchester?'

'It's fine.' She could tell he was disappointed but what did the décor matter? Anticipation built as she followed him up steps to a row of look-alike balconies. Inside, the main room felt cold and smelled faintly of toilet air freshener.

Nathan did a quick inspection of the

facilities. It was a standard layout, with a look of long use about the furnishings. He opened a door leading from the main room.

'There's a separate bedroom through here.' He indicated a dark room almost filled with a queen-sized bed. 'I'll take the divan in this room.'

Shelby hesitated. Would it sound pushy if she suggested sharing? Later would do. Once he set eyes on the feminine white lace undies, he'd surely get the message?

His back was turned to her, solid and withdrawn, as he stood leafing through home delivery food menus and tour pamphlets. He hadn't even given her a welcome kiss or hug. Even when she'd held his hand at the airport, he'd quickly removed himself. This wasn't going to be as easy as she'd expected. How did you seduce a man? She was the last person to know!

She examined the tiny bar fridge. 'Would you like a whisky? Or wine?'

'Thanks all the same. Do you want to

go out to a restaurant later?'

'Not really. I've done enough dining out lately.'

He didn't reply. Had she sounded conceited? He wasn't offering her a drink so she opened the half bottle herself, and filled a glass with fizzy liquid. It tasted like lemonade and she tossed it down, refilling her glass with the rest of the bottle.

Nathan switched on the TV. A late-afternoon episode of 'Days of our Lives' was showing. Whoever had occupied the room last must have been stone deaf. He pounced on the remote, but it was apparently tuned to that channel and no other.

'Looks like the battery's dead.' He paced the room for a minute, then picked up the menus again.

'I'm pretty hungry. I might go for a walk, and bring back some takeaway.'

When had she last eaten? The past thirty-six hours were a blur. Through the grimy window she could see the afternoon light was fading into dusk.

'While you're out, I'll take a shower.'
'Take your time. I noticed a Kentucky Fried outlet down the road. That'll do?'
She nodded. Before she could add anything, he strode away.
The hot water streaming down her body soothed the weariness she was feeling from the long night without sleep. She understood now why her father had referred to 'cattle class' when she'd decided to travel on economy fare. She soaped herself, letting her fingers linger on her nipples, feeling them peak as pleasure arrowed to the pit of her abdomen. The sexual throb reassured her. She was finally healed. Her body was responsive, and tonight she and Nathan were going to make love. He'd listened to her, he'd understood she was afraid. A wave of giving made her determined that tonight he would see her with new eyes, as a woman who felt desire and could respond.
If he'd given up on her, she'd simply

have to change his mind. She dried herself, sprayed on body cologne and unpacked the lacy underwear — just the kind of thing Jasmine liked wearing. Her friend would be cheering her on, if she knew of the change in Shelby. Donning the scraps of silk and lace, she preened in front of the steamy mirror. A blurry vision of allure looked back. Surely Nathan would get the message now?

The room felt stifling. She tried to turn down the heat, but the rusty old fitting was seized. The central heating vent pumped out warm air from some remote location, and she broke out in perspiration from the hot shower and the alcohol. She'd get dressed later. The bed suddenly looked a good place to be. She could grab a few minutes' shuteye before Nathan came back with dinner. Suddenly she felt she hadn't been to sleep for a week. Not even the hard pillow and heavy quilt could prevent her eyelids from closing, as she drifted into oblivion.

* * *

Nathan paid for the order and walked out into the depressing suburban drift of traffic build-up, fumes and asphalt. But it did feel good to stretch his legs and walk off some of his frustration. Shelby was a mystery. Her whole face had been transformed when she saw him walking through the crowd. She'd given every impression of a woman in love, clinging to his hand, gazing at him with admiration. Well, there wasn't much to admire about Nathan Monroe, as she'd soon find out. He was about to dump her because she'd once been the victim of a horrible experience. She had every reason to steer clear of the hurt she associated with men. And he was about to add to her pain.

It was so simple. All he had to do was accept she was out of bounds, sexually. If he could believe that, they could have a great relationship as friends and business partners. Caity would have a wonderful mother-substitute. Shelby would be happy.

And he would be living a lie. Because he wanted her; had done from the moment he'd first seen her sleeping. He'd eyed her, fantasized about her, fancied her, all those recent weeks they'd shared the house and, on one occasion, a bed. Only the presence of Caity had prevented him from taking his desire further, that night of the storm. In retrospect, thank heavens he hadn't pushed Shelby further than she could go. She'd been quite explicit. She said she couldn't stand the thought of sex. How many ways could you interpret those words?

Telling her wasn't going to be easy. Best to wait until they were back home. All his options were disappearing. He'd thrown in his job, made all sorts of plans that involved her. Boarding kennels. Breeding pedigree Labradors for guiding work. Even joining forces with their neighbor and setting up a riding school. Like a fool, he'd mentioned that idea to Lexi, and she'd told him she'd had similar thoughts. She liked the idea of mutual support and said her sister, a physiotherapist, could help draw up programs for disabled riders.

'Nobody else wants old horses,' she'd said. 'But the ones here are slow and gentle, and still have years of useful life.'

His idea of pooling energies seemed natural to her. It was the Asian way, to share the responsibilities of caring for the old and the young. Her grandfather was clearly too frail now to consider taking him back to Vietnam. She would find it so much easier to care for him if other people were nearby.

'Ông Ngoai's recent accident would never have happened if I'd had anyone to watch him while I was out in the paddocks.'

He could see her point. Even today, her help with minding Caity and the dogs saved him having to rush Shelby into a long drive, when she must be exhausted from that long flight. They might have made a great team, Nathan, Shelby and Lexi, each working at a job they loved and helping one another into the bargain.

An old V8 blowing exhaust fumes burned past, fouling the air. So much for the city. He and Shelby would drive back first thing tomorrow. Somehow he couldn't get past that thought.

Back at the motel, he dumped the dinner boxes on the bench and noticed the half-open bedroom door. She must be resting. It was barely five o'clock. How was he going to pad out the hours until he could face that lumpy divan bed?

'Shelby?' The scent of fried food was seeping into the air. He went to call her to eat.

She was sound asleep, one hand under her cheek, like a little girl. But the woman on the bed was no little girl. She'd thrown off the heavy quilt and lay revealed, a vision in white lace. Was she intending to torture him? She was the epitome of purity, yet so alluring he had to physically hold on to the door frame to stop himself lying down beside her. If ever a woman was asking to be ravished, here she was. Had she any idea what effect her half-clad body and sprawled limbs had on him?

He couldn't possibly wake her. She would know he'd seen her and desired her. He turned to step away and close the door when she opened her eyes. For a moment she seemed disoriented. Then she stirred and murmured his name.

'Nathan?' He heard invitation in her soft voice. He must be dreaming. Could she possibly be opening her arms to him?

* * *

The man she called her soul mate was here. Shelby remembered she was home, if home meant belonging with Nathan. Why was he just standing there in the doorway, looking at her? The dregs of sleep ebbed as she gazed back at him. She'd imagined this a dozen times while she'd been away. Now, time was about to make that fantasy real.

Still he made no move. She opened her arms, inviting him. At once, his expression intent, he strode to the bed, kicked off his shoes, tugged off his shirt and lay down beside her. Cradling her against him, he breathed deeply as he softly stroked her fine hair and trailed his fingers along the sensitive skin of her forearm. Tingling pleasure shot through her nerves. The solid feel of his body, his warmth and male scent engulfed her. She reached up and stroked his hair, then sinuously stretched out, letting his gaze roam over her lithe body clad only in its erotic scraps of lace. His Adam's apple moved in the column of his strong neck as he swallowed. Lowering his head, he began to feather tiny kisses up and down her throat.

What was he saying? She couldn't make out his husky words, but through fabric she felt him, thick and urgent. She tugged at his belt, helping him drag off the rest of his clothes. She was submitting to feelings she never knew existed. His fingers fondled and caressed, drawing out her inarticulate moans of pleasure. Slowly he unhooked her bra and eased her small breasts free. The wet friction of his tongue on her peaked nipples made her gasp. Deep in her pelvis, heat built as, immersed in sensation, she flung back her arms and stretched out like a waking cat.

Nathan heaved her onto her side, pulling her hard against his hips until she felt the intimate contact of his arousal. With moist fingers he kept pulling up her nipples then rubbing them flat with the palm of his hand. He nuzzled the nape of her neck, his tongue and teeth flicking shocks of pleasure in her abdomen. He urged her with touches, insisting she was a beautiful, sexy woman.

His hand tugged down the lacy briefs and sought between her legs, discovering the apex of her desire. She was floating in unknown sensation, so compelling yet so strange she tried to escape him.

Disjointed thoughts invaded her mind. Nathan seemed to guess she was struggling but did not take his hand away.

'Just relax, darling,' he murmured. 'Let it go.'

His rhythm changed then, quickening, her breathing fast and shallow as arousal built. Evidently, he would hold his own desire back, and would not relent until she was swept into the depths of pleasure.

'There! Just there!' He was taking her over some unknown peak, and like a dam bursting, all her feelings gathered and spilled over, flooding her with sensation.

Gasping, she opened her eyes and saw him smile. No need now to wait. He positioned his body over hers, seeking entrance. She was slippery and willing. But why was he pulling away? Didn't he want her? With a groan he whispered something. She understood he was reaching for his trousers to retrieve a condom from the pocket. He gazed into her eyes and she saw his expression, filmy with desire, as he positioned himself against her. Had she heard him say, I love you? She felt a moment's discomfort and tensed, until the heavy pounding in her heart overpowered all thought. The room slowly came back into focus. Her first thought was, I'm normal! And a feeling of joy crept through her body. Beside her, Nathan seemed to be recovering. He lay still, his eyes closed, his breathing gradually slowing.

Shelby lay adjusting to the new experience of a lover by her side. She should be tired. Yesterday she'd been in London. She was jet-lagged and had just been through a shattering experience. But hormones still pulsed through her bloodstream, filling her with energy. The moon was full, its silver light penetrating the drab curtains and falling on his face. How much she had to learn about him! Just a few months ago he'd been the distant stranger on the beach, decisive and heroic. Living with him, she'd come a little closer, learning about his haunting loss and concern for Caity. She'd seen he was easy-going, kind, and definitely sentimental, immersing himself in the emotional dramas and glorious music of opera.

Tonight they'd moved to a brand-new place. The physical side had been amazing but, in a way, that wasn't so surprising. Perhaps she'd never understood why sex was so important, but clearly the world disagreed and she'd been prepared to believe the problem lay with her. No, it was the emotions she'd felt that stunned her. Yesterday she'd been a separate being, ten thousand miles away from Nathan. Tonight's joining was a secret, very private contract, binding her to him as a couple. She loved him. She had no doubt of that. Had Nathan said he loved her? It was easy to imagine words she longed to believe.

He sighed, turned to face her, and love shone in his gaze.

'Thank you for saving me,' she whispered.

Nathan pulled her against his naked body, hugging her close.

'I was in the right place, at the right time,' he murmured. 'It was luck. I needed saving too.'

'So did Caity. And Lily. And Skip.' Shelby was struggling to stay awake. 'We all needed saving.'

'I'm just happy we're together.'

'Yes. We're together.' She slurred the words. 'I'm so hungry,' she murmured, but within ten seconds she was fast asleep, and did not stir until the rattle of curtain rings and the hum of traffic penetrated her consciousness. Sunshine streamed in through the window.

'Your coffee, ma'am?'

Nathan, already up and dressed, was smiling down at her as she blinked. A reflex shyness made her pull the rumpled sheet over her exposed breasts.

'Mustn't catch a cold.'

She responded to his teasing by waving the navy boxers she'd uncovered.

'Would these happen to be yours, sir?'

'So that's where they got to?' He set

the cup on the bedside table and sat down, taking her hand. 'I guess you're hungry?'

'Starving.'

He grinned. 'Fancy last night's cold fried chicken?'

'Thanks, no!' She drained the cup. 'I need a shower first, then breakfast.'

'We'll pick something up on the way. I was planning to hit the road by nine.'

'What time is it now?'

He checked his watch. 'Ten-thirty.'

Shelby leaped out of bed. 'Why didn't you wake me?'

'And disturb Sleeping Beauty? We've plenty of time.'

She liked the sound of those words.

Yes, she had all the time in the world to be with Nathan and Caity, forming a new relationship as a family.

Epilogue

'He's a good-looking man,' Shirley commented to her daughter, and Shelby smiled at her.

'I've noticed, Mum.'

She stood by the gate with her parents, waiting as the two riders emerged from the trees and headed along the newly-cleared trail beside the creek. Nathan, relaxed and masterful on Blade, went ahead, guiding Caity on a leading rein. Even from a distance, the little girl's pride and pleasure showed. She was carefully obeying orders, holding the reins with low wrists and gripping her pony's sides with her knees, though the gentle old horse was in no danger of breaking into a canter, and followed Nathan at a docile walk toward the newly-fenced arena.

'Show Daddy your ring, darling.'

Andrew admired the solitaire, its

facets shooting darts of brilliant color where they caught the sunlight.

'Have you set a date yet?'

'We're not in any hurry. This might sound silly, but we haven't had time!'

The past year had been so busy, once the decision to pool resources with Lexi was made. There'd been legal agreements to draw up, and selling Nathan's Queensland property had involved several trips north to clear out his personal property and attend to further legal paperwork.

'Wise not to rush into things.' Andrew put an arm around her shoulders. 'Of course we'll give you a slap-up day.'

He was being protective, as usual. Somehow she didn't mind. She was lucky to have parents who cared.

'We may not want a big wedding, Dad,' she warned him. Nathan wasn't the type of man to be concerned with impressing people. And Shelby couldn't see herself as the center of some huge social turn-out. A few close friends would be enough.

'You said Jasmine's engaged too?'

'She's going to settle in New Zealand with her fiancé. The horse Nathan's riding belongs to her. She's leaving him with us.'

'She knows he'll have a good home. Did you ever imagine you'd both be getting married so young?'

'Not that young, Mum! I'm twenty-three. Didn't you marry at nineteen?'

'That was different. When we met, I just knew Andrew was the one. And that hasn't changed.'

'It had better not!' Andrew kissed her cheek and they shared a private glance. It was the kind of loving moment that used to leave Shelby feeling excluded. Now she just smiled as Caity came running toward them.

In the past year the little girl had blossomed. Secure now in the knowledge that she had a family again, she had started school, and her tantrums were a thing of the past. She was inches taller, and her features had lost all trace of her babyhood. Springy dark curls straggled from under her riding helmet, framing cheeks rosy from exercise.

'Did you see me? Daddy says I can learn to trot soon!'

'You're a very clever girl. I wish I could ride a horse. I was never allowed,' said Shirley, and Caity looked concerned.

'Why?'

'My parents thought I might hurt myself.'

Caity gave a sympathetic nod. 'My daddy was very cross when I rode on Lexi's pony. But now he's teaching me. It's really fun.'

Confined behind the fence, Skip and Lily were missing the entertainment and started a chorus of demanding barks.

'Can they come and play here?' Caity pleaded.

'No, they frighten the horses,' said Shelby. 'They think it's a game to chase them. Once the new house is finished, we'll make sure we have secure fences.'

'Are we ready for the guided tour?'

Nathan walked over and offered his hand to his future father-in-law in an old-fashioned gesture of courtesy.

'I can see you've laid out the plans and started on the footings for the house.' Andrew sounded impressed as Nathan began to list the development he envisaged.

'We'll open a general riding school to start off. And when our partner's sister joins her, she and Lexi are going to handle a disabled riders' program. I'll provide the veterinary service to the horses. We have to make sure we fully comply with the Animal Welfare Code and the Occupational Safety and Health Act. There's the Fire Safety Act, too.'

Andrew gave a nod of approval. 'In a different field, I try to stay on top of the profession. Provide a first class broking service and the clients keep coming. There are a lot of hucksters out there.'

'I know. Some stories are shocking. I've seen some bad cases of animal abuse. I'd like to set a precedent for a well-managed enterprise.'

'And what's my daughter's part in all this?' As they walked across the paddock toward the footings of a sprawling house, Andrew gave Nathan a look of sharp appraisal.

'Whatever she chooses. Boarding kennels are the most likely venture, given Shelby's love of dogs. She's always got a vet on call! I can tell you one thing — they'll be so spoiled they'll never want to go home!'

Andrew laughed. 'That's our Shelby.'

The men strode ahead. Shelby walked with her mother, watching Caity in her riding boots as she kicked at clods of turned-over ground.

'I want you to meet Lexi, Mum. This is her grandfather's land. We're leasing it, and we'll build a separate cottage close to our place, so we can help each other.' She explained how handy it would be to have a baby-sitter right next door, while an extra pair of hands would help with Ông Ngaoi's supervision.

'You seem to have it all worked out,' her mother suggested. 'You know, Shelby, we used to worry so much about you. And now I see a beautiful, confident young woman in love, just starting out on a wonderful life.'

'With a wonderful man,' Shelby reminded her.

'Yes. With a wonderful man. Just like your father.'

'No, Mum. Not a bit like Daddy.'

Shelby smiled, thinking of certain intimate moments one certainly didn't discuss with one's parents. She expected Shirley to blush a little. But her mother laughed. 'I see. Like mother, like daughter.' And arm in arm, they walked on to meet their men.

Other titles in the
Linford Romance Library:

GRACIE'S WAR

Elaine Everest

Britain is at war — but young Gracie Sayers and her best friend Peggy are determined they will still have fun, enjoying cinema trips and dances with Peggy's young man Colin and her cousin Joe. However, there is something shifty about Joe, and Gracie finds she much prefers Colin's friend, the kind and decent Tony. Then, one night, a terrible event changes everything. Now Tony is away at war — and Gracie is carrying the wrong man's child . . .

CUPCAKES AND CANDLESTICKS

Nora Fountain

When Maddy's husband Rob suddenly announces that he's leaving her and moving to Canada with his pretty young employee, her world comes crashing down. As Rob's promises of financial support prove worthless, Maddy finds herself under growing pressure to forge a new life for herself and her four children. She decides to start a catering business, but will it earn enough money — and is that what she really wants? And then she meets the gorgeous Guy in the strangest of circumstances . . .

FLIGHT OF THE HERON

Susan Udy

On her deathbed, Christie's mother confides to her daughter that she has family she never knew existed — grandparents, a great-aunt, and an uncle — and elicits a promise from Christie to travel to Devon to meet them. When she arrives, she's surprised to find another man living there: the leonine and captivating Lucas Grant. But when her grandmother decides to change her will and leave Christie a sizeable inheritance, it's soon all too evident that someone wants to get rid of her, and both her uncle and Lucas have a motive . . .

THE DAIRY

Chrissie Loveday

Georgia is the rebellious eldest daughter of George Wilkins, managing director of the family business, Wilkins' Dairy. Studying for a degree in art, she has become involved with a fellow student, Giles. Following lunch with him and his eccentric artist mother, she ends up moving in with them — but finds it hard adjusting to such a dramatically different lifestyle. Meanwhile, George is struggling with difficulties of his own at the dairy. Can father and daughter both deal with their troubles and find contentment?